The Need to Belong

Callie Bethel

PublishAmerica
Baltimore

PublishAmerica has allowed this work to remain exactly as the author intended, verbatim, without editorial input.

All characters in this book are fictitious, and any resemblance to real persons, living or dead, is coincidental.

ISBN: 1-60672-123-2
PUBLISHED BY PUBLISHAMERICA, LLLP
www.publishamerica.com
Baltimore

Printed in the United States of America

Dedicated to my parents, who believed in me and have always been there for me. To Shasta, who is the best friend I could have ever asked for, and has always been my number one fan. Foremost to God, who has made my dream a reality, and never gave up on me.

Chapter One

All kids have dreams of what they want to be when they grow up. They don't think about it being their job necessarily for life, but as some fun game to play. Kids are brought up playing games, like doctor or school, preparing them for the eventual decision, for what they want to do for the rest of their life. This decision is one that will change your life forever. For some this can be the most difficult decision to make, and for others the easiest. For me this decision was going to be one of the hardest. I had no clue what I wanted to do, I just knew that I was going to choose something, and go to college to be whatever it might be. I heard all the lectures and statistics of the amount of kids who didn't go to college, and how horrible their life was. I defiantly didn't want to be a statistic.

Throughout my life, I wanted to be a teacher, an archeologist, a model, and many other jobs that were unrealistic, as told to me by my elders. It wasn't until my freshman year, that I started writing stories just to pass the time. Some thought it was lame, and others told me I was a great writer. I wasn't the type of person to listen to what others told me though. I wanted the truth, and not many people would actually give me a non-biased answer. I kept writing all throughout high school, and I still had no clue what I wanted to be. Junior year, we had to make some sort of decision, whether we were prepared or not. I decided that it would be easiest for me to just go along with what my family wanted, and be a doctor. My whole family was happy, that I had decided to follow in their footsteps. I tried to convince myself that it was what I really wanted to be, even though in the back of my mind, it was far from it.

Over the next year, everyone always asked me, "Is this what you really want to do?" I always replied with a confident yes, when in all reality, I was anything but confident about my decision. I didn't want to disappoint my parents, my family, and my teachers so I kept on with my fake dream to become a doctor. Senior year, I was still writing at an ever-growing pace. My friends encouraged me to keep writing, and they loved it when I would put them into my books.

One day I finally got up enough nerve and told my best friend, Sophie, that I didn't want to be a doctor, I wanted to be a writer. She encouraged me to pursue my dream, and to actually become a writer. In my world, a dream was all it could be. No matter how much I wanted to be a writer, it would not be good enough for my parents and family. They wanted only the best. Right now, they were so happy that I was going to follow in their footsteps, and be a doctor. I could only imagine their reaction to me wanting to be a writer. To them writing wasn't a career, it was a hobby, and there was no possible way to make a living off it. No matter what they said, I continued to defy them, even though they had no clue that I was.

Graduation was only a couple of weeks away, and I couldn't have been more excited about the pending event. I couldn't wait to get out of high school, and have the whole world at my feet, just waiting for me to go out and make my mark in society. My class like every class before wanted to change the world. One wanted to find the cure for cancer, another wanted to be the President, and many others just wanted to change the world. Unlike my family, my peers believed me to be something great. They believed I would write the next best seller. I had an almost perfect 4.0, I was voted Senior Best Friend and Most Likely to Succeed. I strived to get those things, as it was a competition within my family to see who the best was. I wanted to be the best. I wanted to be the one they were proud of, but I knew that they would never be, if I didn't go to be a doctor like they wanted me to.

As my graduation day neared, my parents started bugging me about which college I was going to go to attend. I was focused on my graduation day, not college. I was always one, who didn't look into the past or future too much. I liked to focus on the present time, and not worry about what may or may not happen. I knew my parents were getting frustrated, with me not making my decision, but I just couldn't make one. I knew that I was going to be a writer, and most likely wasn't going to go to college. Well, at least a college they would count as a college. I had to go to an Ivy League school, to get the best education possible, as my parents reminded me meal after meal. My graduation tickets came in the mail, but there was no fighting over who would get one of the six tickets, like most families. No one wanted to go to my graduation. They said it wasn't as important as college graduation, and there was no real point in going. I was just graduating high school, and that wasn't that big of deal to them, but to me it meant everything. Graduating, high school was the next big step in reaching my potential. My family eventually decided that my grandparents, on my dad's side, my grandma, on my mom's side, and my parents would come. That left one ticket, for me; to give to anyone I wanted. I decided to give it to Sophie. She was after all the only person that I could actually trust and rely on, when I needed her most.

The day of my graduation, she came over to my house to help me get ready.

We kept to the ritual of her doing my hair, and me doing my make up. In these rituals, we would usually talk about guys, the latest gossip, or just talk about our plans for the future. The last subject, we were carefully trying to avoid at all costs. We knew that it would come up, but at the time, we just wanted to enjoy this moment in our lives.

"Claire," Sophie started as she put down the curling iron.

"Yeah."

"What are you going to do about this mess you've gotten yourself into?" She asked me the question I had been dreading.

"I actually have no clue," I paused but then continued. "I want to tell them, but I'm afraid of what might happen if I do." I told her in all honesty.

"What exactly are you afraid of?" She turned me around in my chair so that I was facing her.

"Sophie, you know how our family is. If we do anything to disgrace the family name, they will disown us without a second thought. I cannot imagine not being able to see you or anyone else. Despite our family being what they are, a bunch of one-minded egotistical snobs, I still love them and care about what they think." I said confirming my fear for both of us.

"Well what do you think will happen to me when they find out I want to start my own book store." Sophie said confirming her fear as well.

"We will make a pact right now Sophie. We will never desert the other in their times of need. We will be each other's family. We don't need anyone else but each other." I promised her as we did our secret handshake in agreement to keep our pact.

"I can't wait till I graduate next year." Sophie told me smiling as she continued with curling my hair.

"Make sure you save me a ticket." I told her smiling.

"Don't worry I will." We then heard a knock at the door and it opened revealing my mother.

"Are you two almost done?" She asked us tapping her foot.

"Almost mom." I told her as Sophie finished curling my hair.

"Good, be downstairs and ready in five minutes." She told us emphasizing each word by pointing her handbag at us.

"And I thought my mom was bad." Sophie and I laughed before I quickly grabbed my graduation gown, hat, and cords. Sophie handed me my purse and I slipped on my shoes before we ran downstairs to meet my parents, who were standing at the door impatiently.

"About time girls, we're going to be late." My father snapped as he grabbed his coat and walked swiftly out the door, my mother right behind him. I looked over at Sophie, rolling my eyes, before following them out as well.

When we reached my school I quickly jumped out, glad to get out of the silence. I looked around to see my fellow classmates heading toward the school, trying to figure out what exactly we were supposed to do. I glanced over at Sophie before hugging her quickly and heading into the school. I quickly found some of my friends and ran over to them. We quickly embraced gushing over the fact that we were finally graduating. Before I knew it, we were told to get into the lines, so we could head out. I rushed over to where I was supposed to be and flagged down Dylan, who was beside me in the line up. He smiled and thanked me before taking his place in line next to me.

"Nervous?" I turned to look over at Dylan.

"Yeah, you?" I asked as I heard the graduation march start.

"Of course. Claire, incase I don't see you afterwards, I'm going to miss you, and I wish you all the luck in the world."

"Thanks Dylan. I'm going to miss you too, and good luck with everything." As Dylan hugged me tightly, I felt a tear fall down my cheek. When we separated, I quickly wiped away all evidence of the tear moving forward in the line. Just as we reached the doors getting ready to head out, I looked over at Dylan and smiled encouragingly. I walked out of the door my head held high and a big smile on my face. My hands were shaking slightly but no one could see that except for Dylan, who happened to be in the same situation. When we reached the place for us to separate, he grabbed my hand and squeezed it once. I headed down my row of chairs and stood in front of my seat waiting for the rest of the seniors to make their way into the gymnasium. Once everyone was in front of our seats, we said the pledge and were told to take a seat. They then played our class song and our school song. I tried to stay strong as I saw everyone around me wiping the tears from their eyes as the songs ended. They then introduced our valedictorian June, who gave an amazing speech that made me laugh and want to cry. Once June sat down Victor, our salutatorian came up and gave his speech, which was just as moving. We then had Mike, who our class had chosen, come up and give his speech as well. I applauded with everyone else once all the speeches were done, but I was glad the boring part was over. Our principal then came up to hand out our diplomas. One by one, he called up each row and each person in that row to receive their diplomas and our class flower. Finally, it was my row's turn to walk up to the stage to receive our diplomas like the rest. My row was only second but when you're as nervous as I was, it seemed like an eternity. As I reached the edge of the stage, I hugged the two teachers; we had chosen to greet us. I stood at the edge of the stage waiting patiently for them to call my name. My heart skipped a beat as my principal looked at me and smiled before calling my name. I walked up onto the stage as if on a cloud. It was as if no one else was there even though I heard the cheers of my friends and fellow classmates. As they handed me my diploma, I almost jumped for joy from the excitement I felt rush throughout my body. I smiled brightly as I walked down the stage and got my flower before looking out into the crowd to see Sophie, who was getting glares from our family, but nonetheless was cheering for me. I felt like my face was going to fall off from the amount of smiling I was doing, but I didn't care, this had to be one of the greatest moments in my life. I walked back to my seat and stood in front of it waiting for everyone in my row to come back to their seats, so we could sit down once more. The rest of the graduation went by as a blur, and before I knew it, our principal was congratulating our class, we all stood up cheering and throwing our hats into the air as was tradition. As I made my way through the crowd, I hugged and said my goodbyes to my classmates, as this would be the last time I would ever see them all. Just as I made it through the crowd, Sophie and I raced into each other arms giggling and squealing at the mere excitement of my graduation. I looked behind her to where a graduate would normally see her parents, but mine weren't there. I looked back at Sophie and she told me that they were waiting in the vehicle for us. I sighed and gathered some of my friends together for some group pictures before heading out to the vehicle with Sophie. I climbed into the backseat of the vehicle along with Sophie and closed the door just as it took off.

"It certainly took you long enough in there." My mother said the harshness in her voice obvious.

"Well it was the last time I would ever see them, so I thought I should make the most of it." I said my voice taking the same harshness she used with me.

"You will not take that tone with your mother young lady." My father's voice bellowed throughout the vehicle. I was about to defy them when Sophie placed her hand on my shoulder to stop me.

"This is supposed to be a happy day, don't ruin it." She pleaded with me before I nodded and looked out the window trying to ignore my parent's snide comments.

Chapter Two

That night at dinner, we didn't speak one word to each other. Not even Sophie and me, as we were afraid to break the silence. Sophie and I were about to retreat back to my room when my father told me to sit back down. I had heard this tone in his voice many times, and it was never something to be taken lightly. I immediately obeyed his command, Sophie doing the same out of fear or just the fact she didn't want to leave me. Either way I was glad that she didn't.

"We need to talk about your future." He told me sternly. I sat there not sure, where this was going to lead. I felt Sophie grab my hand under the table for support.

"What exactly do you want to discuss about my future?" I asked in my most professional tone.

"I see you are at least taking this somewhat seriously." My mother commented on my tone.

"Well it is my future we're talking about."

"Have you chosen which university you plan on attending in the fall? The acceptance deadlines are already up." My father continued.

"Well not exactly. Choosing a university means a lot in what type of education I'm going to get."

"The rest of your classmates have chosen already, and I don't see why it is taking you so long to."

"I think it would be in your best interest to go to either Harvard or Yale. After all they are the best, and we expect only the best from you." My mother told me sternly.

"Yes, of course, only the best." I mumbled to myself.

"If you have something to say you are going to say it so that all of us can hear it. Is that clear young lady? You're just lucky we have connections and can still get you into an acceptable school." I only nodded in agreement to my father's command ignoring the rest

"I expect for you to have chosen by the end of this week." He continued before standing up abruptly and leaving the dining room along with my mother.

"If not we will have to choose for you." He said pausing at the door before retiring to their room. I let out the breath I had been holding and slouched down in my chair. Sophie sighed beside me and gave me a look that meant we were going to talk.

"Do we have to talk about this now Sophie?" I whined as she stood up signaling for me to follow. I stood up and followed her outside and to the back of the house.

"You can't be serious Soph!" I exclaimed as I saw her start to climb the ladder leading up to my tree house. When I saw she wasn't I followed her into my one place of solace I had when I was a child.

"I haven't been up here in years." I commented before taking a seat in one of the beanbags on the floor.

"You need to tell them." She said looking up from the floor into my eyes.

"Soph, I'm not ready to."

"When are you ever actually going to be ready to have them disown you?" I saw the fire in her eyes and knew I had to tell them, and I had to tell them soon.

"I know. I told you earlier I'm scared to."

"Well face your fears." She stood up starting to pace the floor.

"If you keep that up you're going to fall through the floor." I joked, but when I saw her face, I knew it wasn't the time for a joke.

"I'm worried about you." She told me in frustration. "I'm worried that I'm never going to see you again, and what they'll do to me when they find out that I don't want to be a doctor either."

"Well." I paused. "I say we're both screwed."

"Claire!" She exclaimed in both amusement and anger.

"I'll tell them Friday night at dinner."

"Claire, that's the family dinner." She said shocked at the very thought.

"Well at least I'll get it all over with at once." I shrugged.

"Claire, you are officially crazy! Do you have a death wish?!"

"No, I'm just tired of pretending I guess." I sighed.

"What are you going to do after telling them?"

"I don't know, but I think you know what is going to happen."

"You can't leave me here." She told me stubbornly.

"If I stay here, they may put me in a mental ward." I joked once again, but by the look on her face, I could tell it wasn't the right time to joke as well.

"Fine. No more jokes." I told her once she had finally sat back down.

"Good, because I don't want to be joking about you being sent to a mental ward." She said cringing at the very thought.

"I'm sure they won't do that. The worst they will do is disown me." I tried to comfort her in some way.

"Is that supposed to comfort me?"

"Yeah." I mumbled.

"Well it didn't. If they disown you…" She trailed off as she started to cry. I walked over to her putting my arms around her in a comforting hug.

"Everything will work out the way it's meant to. We may not think that me being disowned is the best thing in the world, but you never know it might be."

"How can being disowned be a good thing?" She mumbled before looking up at me through her teary eyes.

"I can finally be who I want to be and not worry about what anyone else thinks." I told her trying to looking on the positive side of things. When I did think about it, being disowned might actually be what I need to be able to live my life my way.

"I guess you're right, but I don't want you to leave me." I smiled softly at her as she wiped the tears from her eyes.

"You can call me if you need me, and when you turn eighteen you can join me in being disowned." She giggled and nodded her head.

"Hey girls." I heard a new voice and smiled before looking down to see Jason standing at the bottom of the tree waiting to come up. I motioned for him to come up before sitting down in the beanbag again.

"What are you two up to?" He asked before plopping himself down in the beanbag beside me.

"Well after graduation tonight my parents gave me the ultimatum about choosing a university. So we were discussing how I'm most likely to be disowned when I finally tell them."

"By the way congrats on graduating tonight! The whole disowning thing sucks though, but maybe you can all talk it out and it will work out fine." Sophie and I both glared at him until he raised his hands in defeat.

"Ok maybe talking isn't the best thing with your family."

"No kidding. Remember when I told them that I wanted to take up drums instead of piano."

"Oh yeah! Your mom was like we will not be having you banging on some instrument that has no point whatsoever except to give me a headache." Sophie did her best impersonation of my mother. I laughed as I remembered how furious my mother was that I didn't want to sit around and play classical music all day for her and her friends.

"And when she came home and found out we had a band, and I was the drummer." We all laughed as we remembered that afternoon, which had been the demise of our so-called band.

"We were just getting good too, and she had to go and scare away Allison." Jason laughed.

"How long did you get grounded for again?" I answered her by telling her I had been grounded for six very long months before sighing and leaning back in the beanbag.

"What are your plans for tonight, Jason?"

"Well I was hoping that we could go to the cliffs and hang out." At the mention of our hangout spot, I immediately stood up and dusted off my dress as if saying what are you waiting for. They both laughed and followed my lead down the ladder.

"We'll meet you out front in ten!" I called to him as Sophie and I ran up to my room to change. Once inside the safety of my room, we both found some clothes and quickly changed. We then raced back downstairs, and grabbed our jackets before running out the door.

"Shouldn't we tell your parents?" Sophie asked as we ran toward Jason's suburban, which was sitting out front with Jason leaning against it.

"Like they would even care." I told her before calling shotgun and jumping in the front seat. Jason closed my door and Sophie's before running around to the driver's seat and jumping in and starting up the vehicle. I groaned when we were a few miles away from my house and looked down at my now ringing phone. Sophie looked over my shoulder to see who it was and smirked.

"I told you to tell them." She said in a singsong voice. I turned around and glared at her before answering the phone.

"Hi mom."

"No, Sophie and I are just going to go hang out with Jason."

"Yes, we'll be careful."

"No, we won't stay out too late."

"Yeah, he's right here, mom." I handed Jason the phone and looked back at Sophie before rolling my eyes.

"Yes Mrs. Walker, I will keep them safe."

"Of course."

"Bye Mrs. Walker."

"I think your mother loves me." I glared at him before snatching the phone from his hand and placing it back in my pocket.

"Yeah, she wants us to get married dimwit." Sophie let out a snort before I threw a water bottle that I had found on the floor, at her.

"That could have done some serious damage you know." She said throwing the bottle back at me and sticking her tongue out at me.

"If our parents have anything to do with it we will be married right after college." Jason told me shrugging.

"I'm not going to college though, so this conversation is now over." I snapped at them before looking out the window and nowhere else.

"Come on Claire. It wouldn't be that bad to marry me."

"I'm not saying that Jason. I just don't like how they think they can tell me whom I'm going to marry, and what I'm going to do with the rest of my life." I looked over at him with apologetic eyes.

"It's fine Claire. I didn't take any offense, and I do agree with you about them being a bit controlling."

"A bit!" I exclaimed anger flickering in my eyes once again.

"Ok, maybe a lot." He admitted looking over at me with apologetic eyes.

"Are we there yet?" Sophie whined as if she was a fiver year old on a long road trip.

"We'll be there in five minutes Soph." Jason sighed glad that his conversation with me was interrupted. Sophie sighed and threw herself back against the seat crossing her arms over her chest, acting just like a five-year-old. I looked back at her and couldn't contain my laughter.

"You're acting like you're five, Sophie." I told her still laughing as I looked over at Jason who was trying very hard not to laugh himself.

"But I'm bored." I laughed once again as she whined.

"What's with you tonight, Sophie, you never whine?" Jason chuckled as he turned onto a dirt road.

"I just feel kind of left out." She finally admitted with an exasperated sigh.

"Well you won't be left out once we get there." Jason told her.

"Why?" I asked curiously looking over at Jason, who wore a hint of amusement.

"Oh, you'll find out soon enough." I looked back at Sophie and narrowed my eyes in confusion, but seeing that she had just as much of a clue as I did, I turned back to looking out the window but then decided to look over at Jason. I really had no clue what Jason was planning, but all I knew was that it was going to be something fun. He had a way of knowing exactly what I wanted, and right now, I was in a definite need for some fun to spice up my life. I guess seeing as Jason had been there right beside me since we were in diapers might be a reason to how he knew me so well. I was sad that he couldn't have made it to my graduation, but seeing as he was at his own graduation I didn't think too much of it. I looked over at him and saw that he had really grown up in the time I had known him. He was six feet tall, which always seemed to make me feel short, at only five feet four inches. His curly blonde locks and brilliant blue eyes are what made him quite attractive, not that his body wasn't that bad to look at either. I shook my head and laughed silently to myself as I thought of all the girls who hated me over the years just because they were jealous I was his best friend. I don't really remember how many times I had to assure people that we were only friends and nothing more. I really couldn't think of him as anything else. I looked over at Sophie and had to laugh as I saw her still pouting. Sophie had to be the brunette version of me. Yes, we did have our differences that made us unique, but it was what made us, us. It was funny how all of my friends and I had the exact same color of blue eyes. I sometimes wonder if that was a coincidence or not, but I guess I will never know. Jason's voice snapped me out of my thoughts as he told us that we were there. I glanced over at him and seeing his face, I knew this was going to be a great night. Sophie was practically bouncing out of her seat in anticipation, or just the fact she was happy she could finally get out of the car. She was never one for just sitting in one place for an extended amount of time.

"Well, let's do this." I told them as I got out of the vehicle and was led toward the cliff by Jason as Sophie ran ahead: glad to be out of the vehicle. I glanced over at Jason, as I heard loud voices and laughter ringing throughout the valley.

"You'll find out soon enough, so stop giving me that look." There he went again knowing exactly what I was thinking. As we rounded the corner, I saw a huge bonfire and my closest friends standing around it. I looked around some more and saw there were some tents set up.

"HAPPY GRADUATION!" All of their voices rang out as one. I laughed as Allison finally swallowed her hot dog and shouted it after everyone else. I hugged Jason before running over and hugging the various people there. I couldn't believe that Jason had actually set all this up just so I could get away from it all, and be able to be with all my friends one last time. He knew what I was planning and he supported me fully just like he always did.

"Thought you would want one last night of freedom before you get grounded for life." I smiled at Jason as he led me over to the snack table.

"Let's just hope they only ground me for not doing exactly what they want."

"Claire!" I looked to my left to see a short girl with long blonde hair running toward me.

"Hey Allison." I greeted her with a hug.

"I can't believe you actually graduated."

"Well believe it."

"Hey Claire." A tall curly haired blonde said.

"Elizabeth I haven't seen you in forever." I exclaimed hugging her tightly.

"Brad and Ben are here as well." She mentioned the brothers.

"So are Kayla, Adam, Greg, Chloe, Ethan, and Phoebe." Allison said taking a deep breath as she finished.

"Wow, well. I haven't seen any of those people in a while." I glanced nervously over at Jason before being dragged away to meet all of those people. At one time, all of them were my best friends, but over the years, we had all seemed to drift away from each other. I smiled as politely as I could at the people, which I barely knew anymore. I would have been much more enthusiastic about getting to see all my old friends, but I just had a lot on my mind and I couldn't really seem to focus. Allison and Elizabeth seemed to notice that and decided to drag me off so they could see what was wrong.

"Claire, you're not acting like you usually would." They informed me after giving each other worried glances.

"I'm fine, really. I just have a lot on my mind." I told them honestly.

"Is it because you haven't picked a college yet, because you really need to do that soon or you won't get accepted anywhere?" I glanced at Allison and just nodded my head in agreement. I really didn't feel like getting into an argument tonight with my friends. I had already gotten into an argument with my parents over the same thing, so I just decided to agree and say nothing more about the subject. Allison, however, wasn't going to just let it go.

"I know I don't graduate till next year but you should have chosen a college back in the fall." I couldn't help but glare at her as she ranted on and on about it. I didn't want to say what I was planning on doing, because she didn't know and I didn't want her to know. Allison had this habit of telling everyone what you said. I loved her to death but sometimes I just couldn't for the life of me understand why she insisted on doing some of the things she did. By now, I had tuned out Allison and was just nodding my head in agreement. I was just going through the motions at this point hoping that Jason or Sophie would come rescue me. I looked over at Elizabeth and saw she was bored out of her mind. When she saw I was looking at her she rolled her eyes in frustration. Allison had a way of making anyone frustrated, but for some reason we all still loved her.

"I'm glad we could talk about this but right now I could really use some water." I smiled brightly at her as she nodded understandingly. I walked away from her sighing in relief to get out of that situation. Her views on an education were one of the many reasons why I didn't tell her what I was planning on doing. I hadn't told anyone that I had already been accepted to a college in Colorado. The reason why was I would never be allowed to go to such a small college. This college had a great writing program that I intended to enter. I knew my parents wouldn't pay for it because they would find out I wasn't going to get my medical degree at an Ivy League school. I hadn't even told Sophie or Jason about it yet. I didn't want to get my own hopes up just to have them smashed once more.

"Saw Allison had you cornered." Jason said coming up behind me.

"And you didn't want to rescue me because?" He laughed and handed me a bottle of water.

"I was talking to Brad and Ben." He smiled at me as he saw the glare I was sending his way.

"Where is Sophie?" I looked around the crowd but I couldn't see her.

"I think she went on a walk that way." He said pointing to a trail that led to the cliff.

"I think I'm going to go check on her." I grabbed another bottle of water and started to follow the trail as Jason went back to talking with the guys. I always made sure I gave him some guy time. I knew most of his time was spent hanging out with me, so I always made sure he was able to get away from my craziness occasionally. I hadn't realized how dark it actually was until I was on the trail. I mentally scolded myself for not bringing a flashlight. I had no clue where I was going, because of the darkness, so I just walked toward which direction I thought would get me to the cliff. When I finally saw a dim light up ahead, I almost did a little dance in celebration.

"Sophie!" I called out to her hoping that she would answer me. I waited in anticipation for an answer but to my surprise, I did not receive one. I furrowed my brow in apprehension and started walking slowly toward the dim light. I emerged from the tree line to find nothing but a flashlight lying discarded on the rocks. I looked around and called out trying to find her but to no avail, I took out my cell and called her. I heard her cell ringing to my right so I followed the ringing and found her cell discarded by a bush. I picked it up and placed it in my pocket before calling Jason.

"Jason," I paused as he said his regular hello. "I can't find Sophie. I found her flashlight and cell but I can't find her." I finished in one quick breath.

"Whoa calm down and I'll be right there." I sighed before hanging up and sitting down placing my head in my hands in frustration. I had no clue what had happened to her and it was starting to worry me. If something bad happened to her, I don't know how I would be able to deal with it along with everything else going on. I looked up when I heard a twig snap to my left.

"No one has seen her." I let out another sigh of relief as I heard Jason's voice. He quickly helped me up and gave me a hug.

"So where did you find her flashlight and cell?" I quickly recalled where I had found both.

"Let's try looking for her in this direction." I nodded in agreement and followed him beyond where I had found her cell phone.

17

"Should I call the rest and ask them to help look for her?" He nodded and I quickly called Allison and told her what was going on and to tell the others to help look for Sophie. I glanced over at Jason and saw the worry on his face. I actually had no clue how I was taking this all so calmly. I guess this was just another front I put up. I decided to stop thinking about what could have happened to her and tried to focus on finding her.

"Stop thinking about what could have happened to her." I told Jason, as I knew he was thinking the same way I had been.

"You're right." He let out a frustrated sigh and ran his hand through his unruly, curly hair.

"SOPHIE!" Once more, I called out trying to get some sort of recognition from her. When I didn't hear an answer once more I threw a rock, I had picked up along the way, into the forest. I then heard someone yelp in pain. I winced as I realized I had hit someone with it. I called out an apology sheepishly and turned to look at Jason who was trying to hide his laughter. I playfully smacked him on the arm and shook my head. I didn't know at that time but that would be the last time I would smile that night or for that matter a very long time.

Chapter Three

We never found Sophie that night or the many days like that to follow. No one had a clue what had happened to her, but I wasn't going to give up hope on her, at least not yet. Every day from sunup to sundown, I was out with Jason looking for her. The detectives had stopped the search about four weeks after that night and deducted that she was just another runaway or abduction and there would be no chance we would see her ever again. I hated how everyone just automatically thought the worst in these types of situations. I don't know how they were able to make it through every day with that type of outlook. The only thing that was getting me through the days was my hope that I would see her once again. The only person that hadn't given up hope besides me was Jason. My family and friends once again criticized me, but this time it was for still looking for her. My parents wanted me to move on and just focus on college. I had finally given in and let them enroll me at Harvard in the best medical program they had. I was heading in every generation's footsteps before me, but I didn't even have a clue that this was happening to me. Once again, I was just going through the motions. I was just an empty shell of what I once was. Sophie's disappearance had hit me hard and no matter what everyone tried to do, to get me back to whom I once was, wouldn't work. I was stuck in this mind set and I couldn't see a solution or an end to the pain.

The whole summer had passed by and I didn't even get to enjoy my last days of freedom from life. Somewhere in all of the chaos, Jason had decided to go to Harvard with me. I didn't know if he was just doing this to keep an eye on me or if he actually wanted to pursue the dreams, his parents had for him. About a week before my departure, I woke up and snapped out of the daze I had been in. I heard a knock at my door and quickly got out of my bed to answer it. On the other side was Jason, the only one that had not given up hope on not only Sophie but me as well. It all hit me at once and I couldn't stop the tears that began to pour down my face uncontrollably. I threw myself into his open arms and felt safe once more. He was able to tell me everything that I needed to hear to make me realize what I needed to do, to once again fill the empty shell I had become.

"I feel like I've missed so much." I told him, as I finally was able to stop the tears.

"Don't worry I'll fill you in on everything." He comforted me in the only possible way he knew. It was then that I realized he had tried to take Sophie's place in my life as well as keep his own. It had been possibly harder on him this summer than it was on me. Instead of losing one friend, it was as if he was losing two, Sophie and me. During this whole fiasco, he had to keep a level head and he never once ceased to do just that.

"Thank you. Thank you for everything." I thanked him the only way I knew how. I knew there would be no possible way for me to repay him for all I had put him through this summer. I felt guilty for putting him through everything that I had.

"Don't feel guilty." When he said that I knew he had been able to see through the constant front I put up. I smiled a weak smile and once again placed myself back into the only place I now felt safe, his arms.

"Do you want to go look for her today?" It was a simple question that took a lot of thought to actually answer.

"One last time." I finally told him as he just nodded respecting every decision I was making and would be making to go along with that simple but a complex answer. It was then that I knew he would follow me to the ends of the Earth if I wanted him to. I watched him as he went to sit at my desk. I ran over to my dresser and grabbed some clothes before heading into my bathroom to change. I found it ironic how the clothes I had chose to wear were the same ones I had chosen that very same day that I had lost her. I took a deep breath as I emerged from the bathroom. Jason looked up, glanced down at my clothes, and nodded in some sort of understanding. I wasn't sure myself what that understanding was, but I hadn't been able to grasp most things that had happened to me these past couple of months.

"Ready to go?" I was only able to nod as he led me out of my bedroom and down to the dining room. When we entered, my parents didn't even glance up from their meal. I coughed hoping to get some sort of recognition from them.

"I don't know why you're still even looking for her." My father said not even looking up at me.

"She's gone Claire. Everyone else has already dealt with the fact that she is. Even if it is your fault that she is gone you need to get over it and move on. You can't be going around in a daze while at Harvard." It was then that I remembered why I had been in a daze this entire time. I felt Jason's grip on my waist tighten considerably. I put my arm on his shoulder to calm him. My parents and my family had blamed me for her disappearance. That was how they were able to get over it. Yes, I had been responsible for her, but that didn't mean I could actually control what happened.

"I just thought you should know I'm leaving." I turned to walk out the door but paused not even bothering to face them. "For the last time." Jason then led me out the door, so I didn't have a chance to see my parent's furtive glances or hear their comments that followed. I walked out to his suburban and hopped in the passenger seat closing the door behind me. It was then that the images of that night hit me all at once. I turned and saw Sophie sitting in the backseat laughing at something Jason had said. The sound of Jason closing his door brought me out of the past and back to reality. I glanced back to see nothing in the seat where Sophie had sat just moments before. As Jason pulled onto the road, I felt something hit my foot. I picked it up, and saw it was the bottle that Sophie and I had been throwing at each other. Once again, I was tossed into a memory I didn't want to revisit. Jason's hand on mine brought me back once again. I let the bottle slip out of my grip and I glanced over at him to see the worry that his face was now displaying. I couldn't even bring myself to smile at him to reassure him I was fine. I wasn't going to lie to him and let him believe I was fine when I was far from it.

"Are we there yet?" I was once again thrown into a memory as I asked it. I could hear Sophie asking the same question then me telling her that she was acting like a five-year-old. I shook my head trying to rid my head of those thoughts. I couldn't believe some of my last words to her were telling her that she was acting like a five-year-old. I knew I couldn't change the past but I wished in that moment that I could. I looked over at Jason as we reached our destination.

"Are you sure you're ok?" I shook my head but still proceeded to get out of the vehicle and walk toward the cliffs. I barely heard Jason calling after me. When I reached the cliffs, I let myself fall down onto the hard rock. I sat and stared out at the valley and mountains just beyond. I didn't even feel Jason sit down beside me and wrap his arm around me protectively. I knew he was there though because I felt safe once more. I looked at the mountains and remembered how everyone had scoured them looking for some sort of clue to where she was. I laid my head on Jason's shoulder and thought of the many days we had wasted out here just looking for something we would never be able to find. It was then that I prayed to keep her safe if she was still out there somewhere. With everything that had happened, I had forgotten to pray for her. It was then that I felt all my guilt and sorrow disappear. One little prayer to God had done that. I couldn't help but think that Jason was at that moment going through the same thing I was. I looked over at Jason and saw a look I couldn't describe consume him.

"Did you pray?" Once again, this simple question had many different meanings behind it.

"Yes." I didn't know how he knew but I decided that I didn't need to know. I was just happy that he did know.

"I've been praying this entire time for you and Sophie." He finally admitted to me after a couple minutes of dead silence. It was then and there that Jason and I placed everything in God's hands and decided to forget. We would never forget her, but we would forget about the worry and pain that went along with her memory. I don't know how long Jason and I had sat there in complete contentment but I didn't care. I was worry free at this point and was just happy to be in the safety of his arms.

It was nightfall by the time Jason and I were able to bring ourselves to leave our spot on the cliffs. This would be the last time we would be there for a very long time if ever again. The ride back to my house was a silent one. I think we were both just trying to soak in everything that had just happened in that short period of a day. When I entered my house that evening, my parents were waiting in the atrium for me. I placed my hand over my heart in shock as I turned around to see them standing there.

"Have you finally realized you will never see her again?" I could only nod when I heard their uncaring voices.

"You need to start packing. You're leaving for Harvard in a couple days with Jason." I nodded once again and headed up to my room to pack. I was doing what they wanted me to do. I was going to be their pawn and fulfill their dreams. I had forgotten about the other college I had applied to in Colorado up until that point. I knew there was nothing I could do about it now so I decided to just put that thought to the back of my head to be forgotten. I got the luggage from the linen closet and began to put all my clothes in one, and all my essentials in another.

"Claire, are you packing?" I heard my mother's voice from the other side of my door.

"Yes, mom." I answered her in an annoyed tone. I heard her walk away from my door muttering under her breath. I grabbed a photo album and some other keepsakes and placed them in a suitcase before closing it. I grabbed it and dragged it off the bed placing it outside the door before doing the same to the other two suitcases. I knew our maid would come by later and put them downstairs. I didn't really like having a maid because it made me seem spoiled and helpless, but they did have some uses especially when I decided to be incredibly lazy. I closed my door before walking over to my bed and flinging myself onto it. I lay there just staring at the ceiling because I really had nothing better to do. If Sophie was here, I would have called her and she would have come over, but she wasn't. At that thought, I felt my breath get caught in my throat. I really had to stop doing that. I had to stop thinking what if Sophie was here. I couldn't go back and change the past, so I needed to move on. Going to Harvard with Jason was my way of moving on. No matter how much I didn't want to go there, it would at least keep my mind off Sophie. I shook my head trying to rid myself of those thoughts. I decided I had to find something to do to keep me busy. I went over and sat at my desk trying to figure out what to do. I opened a drawer and saw a small wrapped package. I took it out, sat it on my desk, and stared at it. I didn't know how it got there or what it was, but I had an idea who it was from. That was what kept me from opening it immediately. I knew I had to get it over with, so I carefully took off the paper. Inside was a small book. I traced the leather cover, with my fingers, before flipping through it. It was empty except for a piece of paper that fell out onto my lap.

Claire,

I thought you could use this to write your next best seller. I don't know what you'll write in these empty pages, but I know whatever it is it will be great. You are an amazing writer and person, so don't let anyone else ever tell you that you're not. Keep going after your dreams and never give up. I may not always be there with you in reality, but I will always be there with you in your heart and mind. Keep your dreams a reality not a fantasy.

Love Always Unconditionally Forever in Hope,

Sophie

I smiled and felt a tear slip down my face as I read her note. I had forgotten about how she always signed her letters. I never got why she wrote it like that but nevertheless it always made me feel loved. Her note gave me the hope that I had lost. I would find someway to become a writer just so I could fulfill her hopes and dreams she had for me. It would be hard to do that with everyone breathing down my neck about becoming what they wanted me to be. Everyone was pulling me in so many different directions that I didn't even know which way to go. I heard my phone ringing over on my bed waiting to be answered. I took my time walking over to it and took even more time before actually answering it. I sighed and knew I had to answer.

"Hello?" It was a question because I didn't know who was calling. This was a number I didn't recognize. It wasn't even in my area code. No one answered my question.

"Who is this?" I asked the unknown person on the other end.

"Claire?" I finally got an answer but no sooner had I got that answer I heard a click and then nothing as they had hung up. I still had the phone held up to my ear in shock at the voice I had heard. I recognized that voice as Sophie's as soon as I had heard it. I quickly logged onto my laptop and began a search on that area code. The results came up and I knew I had just been hoping it was Sophie. There was no way it could have been her. This area code was a Colorado area code. I sat there staring at the computer screen and my phone trying to figure it out. I decided to call the number back and see what happened.

"Laugh Bookstore how may I help you?" This wasn't the same voice I had heard before.

"Sorry, I have the wrong number." I hung up pondering about what just happened. I decided not to think on it any more and just go to bed. I would need my rest for tomorrow. Jason's parents and mine were taking us out to get stuff to furnish our apartment. Jason and I were going to have adjoining apartments off campus. My parents were able to use their power and fortune to bend the rules for us to be off campus for our freshman year. Evidently, they already had our apartments picked out and we just needed to get all the furnishings for them. I sighed knowing tomorrow was going to be a very long day. I quickly changed into my pajamas and got into my bed, falling asleep as soon as my head hit the pillow.

I woke up the next morning with a loud knock on my door. I groaned as I opened my eyes and saw it was still pitch black outside. I rolled over and covered my head with my pillow, but the knocking then got louder and more persistent. I groaned and answered them by telling them I was up. I slipped out of my bed and jumped slightly as my feet hit the cold wood flooring. I ran toward my bathroom trying to make sure my feet didn't stay on the cold floor more than need be. Once inside I took a quick shower, wrapped myself in a fluffy towel, and went through my room over to my walk in closet. I flung open the doors and walked inside trying to figure out what outfit would be deemed appropriate for shopping with my parents and Jason's. I decided on some nice jeans, a pink, and a white striped polo. I then slipped on some flip-flops and headed downstairs for breakfast. Upon opening my door, I was met with the maid.

"Your mother asked me to see that you're dressed appropriately for the shopping trip." I rolled my eyes and turned around for the maid seeing if she deemed my outfit sufficient for my mother. The maid nodded in approval before walking back down the hallway. I sighed as I heard the click of her heels getting softer. I would never understand my mother's ways. Once I couldn't hear the maid's footsteps anymore, I started walking in the same direction heading down to the dining room. I had waited for the maid to be gone before walking that way myself, because I liked walking alone in these vast hallways. There was just something about them that made me feel like I was in a fairytale and everything was right once again in the world. I skipped down the hallways carefree. Skipping in these hallways had been a tradition I had kept since I was a small child. Once I reached the top of the steps, I placed my hand gracefully on the railing letting it glide on it as I walked down the stairs. These stairs always made me feel like I was a princess going to meet my prince. I took my time to enjoy this because it wasn't very often that I actually got the time to do so. As I reached the doors to the dining room, I placed a hand on each door flinging them open and gracefully walking through them. I loved to make an entrance like that whenever I could. This morning seemed to consist of things I loved to do but never actually got the time to do. My smile slowly faded as I saw my parents, Jason, and his parents sitting at the dining room table waiting. I took my seat beside Jason and placed my napkin on my lap before looking up at the others at the table. Once I had acknowledged each of them, they started the meal. This was one tradition that I hated. I wanted to just come in and eat like a normal family, but seeing as my family was high class that just couldn't happen. I looked over at Jason who was holding back a smile as he took a drink of his orange juice. I looked up to see if our parents were watching before sticking my tongue out at him. He returned the favor but was only scolded by his mother. He always forgot to look before doing stuff like that. I smiled brightly and started on my pancakes. I forgot to mention that my family also has a cook that prepares every meal. Cooking and baking is apparently above my mother. She only likes to prepare parties and functions nothing else. I even had to be a debutante because she was a member in the society along with Jason's mother. Don't get me wrong I love to dress up but I hated going to all of the functions and having to act like a complete lady at all times. Sometimes I couldn't stand some of the other girls in my society. Each girl compared each other by the amount of money you had and how many connections you had. I of course had a substantial number of both but never took part in their bragging rituals. My mother of course did at every chance she got. It never ceased to amaze me how well she spoke of me at these functions, but as soon as she was behind closed doors, she treated me as if I was the exact opposite. I wondered if the other mothers, in the society, did the same to their daughters, that wouldn't surprise me. Most people wanted to be in this type of society, but I wished for the exact opposite. I just wanted to be in a normal family. I shook my head and decided my family would have a normal life, unlike the one I've had to live. I was snapped out of my thoughts when Jason's mother, Daphne, spoke to me.

"Claire, I'm so glad you decided to follow in your parents footsteps, and I'd like to think that you were the deciding point for Jason to follow in ours as well." I just smiled nodded and thanked her. In this type of society, that was a compliment.

"Pull the car around and make sure it's warm by the time we're done eating."
My father told Greg our driver. Yes, we even had a driver. I chewed on my
bacon slowly as everyone else finished their meals. I nodded at the maid as she
took my plate away along with Jason's. Jason and I then sat there waiting for our
parents to finish their meal so we could leave the table. Jason and I waited quietly,
deciding it was best as to not make our parents upset this early in the morning.
Our parents took their time finishing their meal, even after a maid came in and
told us the car was waiting for us out front. I seriously didn't know how my
parents ever made it to work on time with them being this slow. As soon as they
were finished eating, they made their way from the dining room to the atrium.
The maid then brought us our coats and purses and we headed outside to my
parent's black Cadillac Escapade. Jason and I sat in the very back seat and his
parents in the second row and my parents up front. I was glad that Jason and
I were in the back so we could have our own conversation without interrupting
our parents. They would also be so wrapped up in their own conversations that
they wouldn't even notice that we were talking.

"Jason," He looked up and nodded for me to continue. "I found a letter and
book from Sophie in my desk."

"What?" He asked in shock.

"She put it there before graduation."

"Well, what did it say?"

"It just said how proud she was of me and stuff like that."

"You're going to be a writer aren't you?" I just nodded and looked out the
window then back at him again, his eyes had never left me.

"I'm glad you're still going through with it. For a while I thought you weren't
going to anymore." He grasped my hand tightly still staring into my eyes.

"Aww aren't they so cute together?" We quickly jumped apart as I heard his
mother comment on our closeness.

"We're going to be family before we know it Daphne." My mother told
Jason's mom with a big smile on her face. Our parents never gave up on trying
to get us together. For the rest of the ride Jason and I kept our distance from
each other to avoid any more comments from our parents.

When we came to our first stop, Jason and I jumped out of the vehicle and
ran toward the store ignoring our parent's calls. We entered the furniture store
and wasn't there long before the associates immediately came to our side trying
to ensure our happiness. Our parents entered and took off walking toward the
bedding section. Jason and I were quick to follow making sure we kept up. Upon
reaching the section my mother pushed me in toward the girls section and Jason

toward the guys section. I didn't want to spend all day looking so I just chose the first one I came upon that I liked. It was a queen white canopy bed that came with a vanity, dressers, and a desk. I then chose a couple comforters, sheets, and the works to go with it. Jason had evidently chosen the first bed he came upon as well and was waiting patiently for us with our dads. We then went to the dining room and kitchen section choosing everything that we thought we might need. We then went to the living room section and then to the bathroom section. By the time we were finished it was once again dark outside. We arrived in the dark and then left in the dark. The ride home was quite for Jason and me because we had fallen asleep as soon as we got in our seats. I felt someone shake my arm and I slowly opened my eyes to see our mothers' standing over us smiling brightly. I then realized that Jason had his arms around my waist pulling me toward him also his legs were entwined with mine and my head was lying on his chest. I felt really comfortable and safe but I also felt very embarrassed that we ended up like this and our mother's were now fawning over how cute a couple we were. I tried to get out of his hold but when that didn't work, I poked him sharply in the side until he woke up. When he did wake up he quickly let go, pushing himself away from me, and mumbled an apology.

"Why don't we all go in and have some tea and crumpets, Daphne?"

"That sounds absolutely lovely, Cordelia." I got out of the vehicle along with Jason and followed our parents up to the house.

"I'm going up to my room." I told my parents as soon as I entered the house.

"Take Jason with you then darling." I sighed and started walking up the stairs knowing Jason was close behind. I entered my room and went over to my desk laying my head down on it. I heard my door close and Jason walk over to where I was sitting.

"Is this the letter and book?" I heard him say as he picked up the two items in question. I mumbled yes not stopping him from looking at them. He put them back down on the desk before going over and sitting on my bed.

"What are you going to do when we leave in a couple of days?"

"I'm going with you."

"No, I mean do you want me to cover for you or drop you off somewhere?"

"No, I'm still coming with you to Harvard."

"But,"

"Just drop it Jason." I turned to look at him to see him drop back down onto my bed with a sigh.

"I'll figure something out but for right now I'm going to do what my parents want."

"Are you sure?"

"I'm positive. And you never know going to Harvard might be good for me."

"The only thing I'm going to like about Harvard is you." I turned to look at him, but it was too late he was already out the door.

Chapter Four

I sat there just thinking about what he had said. I have no clue how long I had sat there doing just that. I looked at the clock and saw I had been sitting there for three hours. I sighed and got up getting ready for bed. What he had said haunted me in my dreams and thoughts for the next couple of days. I didn't know how to get rid of them, but I don't think I actually wanted to get rid of those thoughts. I heard a knock on my door and looked up from where I was sitting at my desk. My mom came in and sat down on my bed patting beside her. I slowly walked over and sat down next to her.

"Your father and I think your going to do well at Harvard, and we wanted to tell you to make us proud and make sure our family name is well represented." I guess that was her way of having a mother daughter talk with me. I only nodded as she continued to tell me how to act while at Harvard.

"What if I decided I didn't want to be a doctor?" There I had finally said it.

"Well that's just absurd Claire." At least I had tried to get it through to her. I didn't really feel like arguing with her especially since I had so much on my mind.

"Isn't it?" I laughed nervously as she patted me on my knee and got up to leave.

"Jason is a wonderful young man. Maybe you should think on that." She then walked out of my room closing the door silently behind her. I knew she was going to bring that up in a conversation sooner or later. Personally, I had been dreading that moment. Jason was my best friend who just happened to be very attractive. I couldn't like him like that, could I? I felt my stomach drop as I realized that I might have the tiniest bit of feelings for Jason. There was nothing wrong with liking him it was just the fact that I was afraid of liking him or anyone for that matter. I heard a buzz and then heard my father's voice over the intercom.

"Jason is here." I felt a small jolt when I heard his name, but then I realized he was here to pick me up to go to Harvard. I picked up my purse and slipped the journal and letter from Sophie in it before going to the door. I opened it and looked at my room once more before heading downstairs to meet Jason. As I reached the top of the stairs, I saw Jason standing there waiting as my maids took my luggage out to his suburban. I saw him look up and I smiled at him, but he didn't smile back. He turned to my father and shook his hand before hugging my mother and walking over to the door. I continued my journey down the stairs before finally reaching my parents. I gave them both an awkward hug before walking over to where Jason was standing. As soon as I reached him, he walked out the door without even acknowledging me. I guess he is a bit upset with me. He did basically tell me his feelings for me, which I didn't even acknowledge. I guess he thought I had rejected him, which wasn't even the case. I was just too shocked to say anything, but now that I had thought about it I knew what I would say if he ever decided to mention it again. The trip to Harvard was going to be a long one and there was no way he wouldn't talk to me. I smiled thinking about what I would say to him when he finally would bring it up. There was no doubt in my mind that he wouldn't bring it up. I got in the front seat and sat quietly waiting for him to get in so we could leave. When he got in, I felt extremely nervous. I hadn't ever felt this nervous around him as long as I had known him. He started the vehicle and pulled out onto the road, beginning our long journey to Harvard.

For the first hour, I sat looking out the window, but when I finally became bored of that, I turned on the radio. I glanced over at Jason to see if he even noticed, but he didn't even acknowledge that I was there or that I had turned on the radio. I sighed and slumped down in the seat annoyed that he was purposely ignoring me. Yes, he did admit his feelings and was probably too embarrassed to talk to me or he was just being stubborn. I sat there in a daze just thinking about all the different reasons he had for ignoring me. I glanced out the window, saw a rest stop sign, and realized that I had to go to the bathroom. I wasn't sure whether I had been so caught up in my thoughts and hadn't realized it or it was just the power of suggestion that brought it on. I sighed and looked over at Jason, who kept his eyes glued to the road.

"I have to go to the bathroom." I finally said with a huff. He didn't even acknowledge me, but I knew he had heard me because he turned into the rest stop. When he finally parked the vehicle, I jumped out and ran inside. I finally decided that I had to go to the bathroom the entire time but was too caught up in my thoughts. As I emerged from the bathroom, I saw Jason standing by a vending machine trying to get it to take his money. He let out a frustrated groan and kicked the machine. I couldn't help but giggle, but then he turned around and saw me. His facial features stopped showing all emotion and he started to walk back out to the vehicle. I nearly screamed in frustration as he continued to ignore me. I smirked and went over to the vending machine putting in money and getting a drink and something to snack on. I then got the same for Jason and placed them in my bag for leverage later. I couldn't help but let out a small laugh at how evil I was being. It was somewhat silly that I was holding food hostage when he could just stop at a restaurant and get his own food. I walked slowly out of the building and over to his SUV. Taking my time when he wanted to go somewhere usually bugged him. I don't know what exactly possessed me to try to bug him all of a sudden. I think it was just the fact that him ignoring me was actually getting to me, so I was having a little payback. When I finally reached the vehicle, he started it up and took off just as I had closed my door. I put my bag on the floor and fastened my seat belt before getting my soda and chips out of my bag. I saw him glance over out of the corner of my eye, and I couldn't help but smile. I looked over at him to see if he was still looking but he wasn't. I knew he was watching me out of the corner of his eye, so I decided to torture him as much as possible. Jason couldn't go more than a couple hours without eating something. It was one of the annoying habits he picked up from one of his guy friends. I opened the bag of chips and took a chip out agonizingly slow before placing it in my mouth. I saw his hands tighten on the wheel and knew I was at least having some sort of effect on him. I then opened my soda and took a big gulp before placing it in a cup holder. He started to tap his left foot as well as hold onto the wheel tighter. He was trying oh so hard to resist the urge to grab my drink or grab my chips. He was used to just reaching over and taking whatever he wanted without even asking me, but now he felt compelled not to do just that. I decided that eating and drinking in front of him just wasn't enough, so I started to comment on how good they were. It was un ordinary for me to comment on things without even caring if someone listened. The muscles in his arm started to twitch as he listened to me. I know I was being incredibly cruel to him at this point, but I found it fun to watch him literally twitch.

"Oh yeah I got you some chips and a soda too if you want them." I finally told him with a smirk acting as if I had just remembered. I got them out of my bag and set them on the middle console, awaiting him to finally give in and take them. The items in question sat there mocking him until he finally gave in and grabbed the drink. I smirked and tried to conceal a giggle as he chugged down the soda. After he had finished drinking the soda and eating, the chips I had gotten him his eyes glued themselves straight to the highway once more. I huffed in anger, as he didn't even say thank you or one syllable to me.

"You're welcome." I told him even though he didn't say thank you. My eyes widened in anger once more when he didn't even reply to that. I grabbed the book Sophie had gotten me and a pencil, but that was all I got accomplished as I sat there staring at the empty book before me just waiting to be filled with my thoughts, dreams, beliefs, everything and anything I could think of. One thought filled my mind as I sat there staring at the page. Writers' block sucks immensely.

I could have sworn I heard Jason laugh, but it was soon covered by a cough. My eyes narrowed at him before searching around for the pencil I had thrown, which had caused Jason's coughing fit. I found the pencil, but I also had found Sophie's letter. I picked both items up and sat them in my lap. I unfolded her letter and began to reread it. After I had finished reading it, I looked out the window and knew exactly what I was going to write. At this moment, I felt the urge to write my life story. I had no clue why exactly I just felt like people needed to know my story. My life would surely be more interesting than some of the other lame things I had thought up. As the pencil met the paper, the words just came to me as if they had been there all along, and I had somehow found the key to unlock them. I was about 20 pages into the book when Jason pulled off the highway. I glanced up and noticed that it was past lunchtime, so he was probably trying to find a place to eat. It was a small town that didn't have much so he finally stopped at a small burger joint. I placed my book back in my bag and got out of the vehicle following him inside the restaurant.

"Two?" Jason nodded as an older woman led us to a small table for two by the window. I sat down and ordered myself water before excusing myself to the bathroom. When I got back my water and my food was already sitting there waiting. I knew I hadn't ordered any food so Jason had obviously ordered for me. I smiled knowing he still cared enough to order my food. I sat down and saw that he had ordered me chicken fingers and fries, my usual. Yeah, he knew me extremely well. Well at least he paid attention to the things I said and did. I let out a small laugh as I realized he sounded a bit like a girl. Most guys don't really pay attention or notice anything, well at least any normal guy doesn't, but when have I ever labeled Jason as normal.

"Thank you." See I still had enough manners to thank him. All I got from him was a grunt and a nod. I had officially had it with him ignoring me, so I picked up a fry and threw it straight at him. The fry hit him on the nose and landed on his plate. He looked up at me with an annoyed and confused look on his face.

"I've had it with you ignoring me." He sat there contemplating God only knew what before he threw the fry back at me and began to eat once more. Ok, if he was going to still ignore me after that then I was going to have to do something he will most likely hate me for. I grabbed his plate and his fork hit the table as he went in for more food.

"You are not getting this back till you talk to me!" I said in a huff. I saw some of the people in the restaurant look up from their meals to stare at us, but I really didn't care.

"Give me my food back." He said rolling his eyes.

"No." I told him stubbornly as I held his food ransom. "You are going to tell me why you are ignoring me." His shoulders fell and he placed his fork down before looking me straight in the eye.

"Do we have to do this here?" He asked with pleading eyes. I shook my head before grabbing his hand and leading him toward the only place I knew we wouldn't be heard or seen, the bathroom. I entered pulling him in with me and locking the door behind us. He slowly surveyed the place before turning back toward me.

"This wasn't really what I had in mind. I thought we could wait till we were done eating or something."

"Well you thought wrong. I want to talk now." I said starting to pace back and forth in the extremely small bathroom.

"I embarrassed myself." He stated finally.

"No, you didn't." I told him firmly.

"You didn't say anything. In my book that's quite embarrassing."

"You didn't give me a chance." I told him softly finally stopping and lifting my eyes up to meet his. His eyes widened as what I said clicked in his head. It was as if a light bulb went off somewhere in the place between his ears he called a brain.

"What would you of said then?"

"Well considering you was so vague about saying it then, not much." He threw his hands up in frustration and took over my job of pacing.

"But now, I would have to say I feel the same." He stopped mid step and tripped over his own feet as he spun around to face me. I looked up at him sheepishly as he stared at me with a look of shock, amazement, and excitement.

"So what exactly did you get from my vague declaration?"

"Well I think what you were trying to say in your weird sort of way was that you like me as more than a friend. Am I right?" I asked looking at my shoes afraid to look at him.

"Yes." I felt his finger under my chin lifting my head up to look at him. The next thing I knew his lips were on mine and we were engaging ourselves in a fierce battle of emotions. I felt overwhelmed with the emotions spreading throughout my body like a disease. I felt excited, nervous, loved, and every other emotion in between in a matter of seconds. We finally pulled away from each other breathing hard as we stared at the other intensely.

"I think our parents will be extremely happy with this development." He said smirking as his arms tightened around my waist. I blushed but continued to let my fingers play with his golden locks at the nape of his neck.

"This is quite a sudden development." I heard myself say. I could barely hear myself over my heart's rapid beating.

"I don't think it's actually that sudden." I couldn't help but nod in agreement.

"We probably should go back out and finish our meal." He nodded and kissed my lips softly once more before opening the door for me to exit. As we walked back to our table, every eye was on us. I sat down and started to eat again trying to ignore the stares.

"This is getting awkward." I giggled and nodded before taking his hand, which was lying on the table.

"Are we an official couple?" I asked as he rubbed his thumb softly against my hand.

"I would like to think so." I smiled and squeezed his hand before taking a drink of my soda. He finished his meal and waited quietly for me to finish mine before we got up to go pay for our meals. Jason paid for both of our meals before taking my hand and walking out of the restaurant and out to his suburban. He opened my door for me before going around to the driver's side and getting in.

"Is there anywhere you need to go to before we get back on the highway?"

"Is there a store nearby so we can stop and get some snacks?" Jason shrugged before checking his GPS to see if there was anyplace nearby.

"There is a gas station about a block from here, and we might as well fill up while we're at it."

"Sounds good to me." He started up his suburban, pulled out of the restaurant, and headed to where the gas station was supposedly located. Once we made it to the gas station, I went in and got some snacks and drinks for the rest of the trip while Jason started to pump some gas for the suburban. I knew it would take forever to fill it up so I looked around inside and ended up also getting a crossword book, gel pen set, and some souvenir mugs. I went up to the register paid for my stuff and headed out to where Jason was still pumping gas.

"Is it done yet?" I whined after putting the stuff the vehicle. He laughed before shaking his head. I leaned against the suburban next to him, taking his hand in mine. I saw him glance down at our hands before looking back up with a smile. I couldn't help but smile as I felt him squeeze my hand gently. I couldn't help but get butterflies with every little thing he did. I was confused because I had never got butterflies around him before. I guess it was just the fact that I finally realized that I did like him and stopped denying it to myself, and the fact that he was now my extremely handsome boyfriend. Many girls want him, and now I had him.

I giggled as I thought of the looks on everyone's faces back home when they found out we were now an item. I also felt pleasure in knowing that many girls would be mad or just really jealous of that fact. I normally didn't think like that, causing me to feel some guilt, but then I decided I had every right to be happy that Jason was now mine. I mentally scolded myself as I thought that for making him seem like an object. It was then that I realized I was thinking differently than what I have ever before about him. I then remembered all the times I felt a jolt of jealousy every time he had a girlfriend or girls fawned over him. I guess I had liked him longer than I actually thought.

"How long have you liked me?" I know it was a random question, but I just had to know. I looked over at him awaiting his answer, as he stood not moving a muscle.

"Do you remember when we were at your grandparent's farm when we were 12 and you fell out of an apple tree and broke your arm?" I nodded in confusion as to why he was telling me this, but then it hit me.

"I've liked you since then. When I saw, you get hurt I realized just how much I cared about you. It took me a couple years though to actually realize those feelings were more than just feelings of friendship."

"Wow. Why didn't you say anything to me then?"

"I didn't think you felt the same way. When did you realize you liked me?"

"Last night." He gave me a strange look before staring back at the pump.

"I just realized I liked you last night, but I've liked you since we were 12 as well." I saw his eyes brighten as he looked over at me. I smiled and kissed him softly before I heard the click from the pump signaling that it was done.

"I'm going to go pay for this, and I'll be right back." He kissed me and smiled before heading toward the store. I blushed and smiled before getting in the suburban. I couldn't help but smile as I saw him come out of the store looking at me and nothing else. I felt like a giddy schoolgirl, and I actually liked that feeling. I had never felt anything like the way I felt about him in my entire life. I know my entire life isn't that long compared to everyone else in the world, but it felt like a lot to me. I loved Jason as a friend and I liked him as my boyfriend, but I couldn't help but feel like the love I felt for him as a friend transferred over to my relationship with him as my boyfriend. I shook my head as I tried to clear my head of all thoughts. It wasn't that I was afraid to love Jason as a boyfriend, but it was the fact that I was thinking all of these things way too fast. I needed to slow my thought process down, just take things slowly, and not rush these things. I was snapped out of my thoughts as I heard his door close. I glanced over at him and smiled as he started up the suburban and pulled out of the gas station.

Once we made it back onto the high way, I pulled out my journal and began to write in it once more. Maybe my life would be interesting enough to sell as a book. I laughed softly at the thought of my life being able to be sold as a book.

"Do you think my life is interesting enough to sell as a book?" Jason laughed before nodding his head.

"Claire, you do the most amazing things and your family is like a soap opera." I laughed shaking my head as I realized just how much my family was like a soap opera.

"Yeah, true." I smiled before going back to writing in the journal. Right now, I was halfway through my childhood. The first couple of chapters would just be background info for my teenage years. Those years were far by the most interesting and thought provoking. I sighed as I thought about how much my family will detest me for writing an unplugged story about them. My family was extremely well known and respected. Everyone wanted to know how we lived, but I had a feeling that people wouldn't be expecting my version of our life. I had a feeling that more people would want to read my version though. I laughed to myself at the thought of my family reading my book. They would probably pass out from shock after reading the book. Don't get me wrong, but I'm not trying to destroy my family. I'm probably not going to keep any real names, and I'll use some artistic license with the story so it won't really be anything like a biography. I glanced up from the book at the clock and saw we had been on the road for six hours now.

"Do you want a break?" I asked seeing if Jason wanted me to drive for a while.

"Maybe in a couple hours." I nodded and put my book away deciding I had written enough for the day. I got out Sophie's letter again and looked over it again trying to see if she had left any clue to where she had gone.

Chapter Five

L ove Always Unconditionally Forever in Hope." I repeated to myself again
as I tried to get something, anything, out of her letter.
"What's that?" Jason asked glancing over at me.
"Oh, it's just something Sophie always used to sign on our letters."
"So do you have any leads on Sophie yet?"
"Did I tell you about the phone call I got?"
"No, what phone call?"
"A couple days ago I got a phone call from this bookstore in Colorado."
"What does that have to do with Sophie?"
"I think it was Sophie who called. The person on the other end called me
Claire, and they sounded just like Sophie."
"Are you sure?"
"I'm positive. I would recognize her voice anywhere."
"Then what are you going to do?"
"I have no clue. I can't just go on a wild goose chase."
"Do you know anything about the bookstore?"
"Yeah. It's called Laugh Bookstore."
"Well we'll just have to search for a Laugh Bookstore in Colorado."
"What do you mean, we?"
"Did you actually think I would let you do this by yourself?"
"Well no. You want to go searching for Sophie?"
"Yeah, why not."
"Well, what if it ends up that we were wrong, and we do all this for nothing."
"Even if we are wrong, I don't think going to Colorado would be for
nothing."
"Going to Colorado?"
"What did you expect us to do?"
"I don't know. I guess I wasn't really thinking."
"So when do you want to head to Colorado." I looked over at Jason and
stared at him as if he was crazy.
"What?"
"We still have to figure out where the bookstore is, how to get there, and we
can't just not show up to Harvard."

"Well we will go to Harvard, find out all of that stuff then leave."

"Our parents will kill us."

"Since when have you cared about what our parents will or will not do?"

"Never." I finally admitted. A smile found its way onto my face as I saw Jason grinning happily.

"So we're going?"

"Yes, but only after we get to Harvard and rest up some."

"Fine." Jason said a bit dejected like a small child. After Jason and I had finished our conversation about Sophie, I couldn't help but feel the hope I had lost come back to me. I hoped that we would find her, and that she would be ok when we did find her. I don't know what I would do if we never found her after I got my hopes up again. I really didn't want to think about what would happen if we didn't find her. I wanted to focus on just finding her and bringing her home safely. I couldn't help but wonder where our real home really was. Was it in West Virginia with our parents, Harvard at school, or wherever the road may take us? I thought back to before she disappeared and how I was going to do just the same thing. It wasn't my goal to get away from my parents and start my own life, but to now find Sophie and start our own life together with Jason. I wasn't completely sure on the Jason part even though I wanted to be sure of it. I never really thought about Jason being in my life. Yes, he was always in my life but not in the same way, I'm thinking now. It's amazing how things can completely change in a matter of seconds, minutes, or even hours. My whole life has changed so much in the past couple of months since Sophie came up missing, Jason and I left for Harvard, Jason and I are now in a relationship. I have to say months and not days because of my disappearance from the earth. Yes, my disappearance not only Sophie's but mine as well. When she left a part of me left with her and I was in a state of mind that very few would be able to get me out of. I'm just glad Jason was able to do just that. He was kind of like my knight in shining armor and I couldn't wait to tell the world just that.

"You ready to switch so I can take a nap?" He once again brought me back from being lost in my thoughts. I nodded as he pulled over to the side of the road where we switched places. I hated driving at night because my mind always seemed to take me to different place and time. I really didn't want to do that now so I got my ipod out of my purse and turned it on to distract me from my thoughts. I also decided to open the window to let in some fresh air. It was amazing how dark it could get in such a short amount of time. I wasn't one to be afraid of the dark but more along the lines of what is in the dark. I tried not to focus on what could be in the dark as I drove along the highway. I checked my watch and saw it was almost ten o'clock. I glanced over at Jason to see him sound asleep. I really didn't know what to do about the whole Sophie situation, but my mind kept drifting to what Jason had said. Maybe he was right, maybe we should go to Colorado and try to find her. I had no clue how we were going to get there, but I couldn't help but want to at least try to find her. I snapped out of my thoughts as I heard a phone ring. It was Jason's phone that was lying in the center console. I looked over at Jason and knew he wasn't going to wake up anytime soon. I paused my ipod and grabbed his phone to answer it. I didn't bother looking at who was calling but just answered it.

"Hello?"

"Claire! Hi, it's Daphne."

"Oh, hi. I don't mean to be rude, but is there a reason you're calling?"

"Yes, Darien is in the hospital." My eyes widened when I heard Jason's dad was in the hospital.

"What happened?" I asked as calmly as possible. I reached over and shook Jason trying to rouse him.

"He was starting the fire in the living room when it blew up in his face. He has third degree burns all over and is in critical condition." This was the first time I had ever heard Jason's mom this concerned about anything. That is what really worried me the most.

"We'll come home right away."

"No, you two need to go to Harvard."

"Darien is more important than Harvard. It doesn't matter if we're a bit late."

"Yes, it does. I will not have you two disgrace our good names by being coming and going when you please. It's incredibly irresponsible." I sighed and shoved the phone into Jason's chest as he finally woke up.

"Your mother." I told him as I pulled over to the side of the road.

"Mom, calm down."

"Claire and I are heading home right now." He hung up the phone and I did a U-turn in the road heading back the way we had just came.

"Jason…"

"I don't want to talk about it Claire." I nodded silently and looked back at the road in front of me. It would only be about seven hours back to West Virginia if we didn't make any stops. It had taken us about eight and a half hours to get to New York because of all the stops we had made. I just hoped that I wouldn't get lost on our way back. I couldn't read maps very well and Jason's GPS was freaking out on me because I had strayed from the course. I didn't know how to reprogram it either, so I was pretty much on my own here. I wasn't going to ask Jason for help as he was in a daze right now. I glanced over at Jason to see him staring out the window his head leaning against the window.

"He'll be fine Jason."

"You don't know that, so don't say it." I opened my mouth to say something but closed it just as quickly as I had opened it. Right now probably wasn't the right time to say anything to him. I looked down at the GPS, which kept flashing 'wrong way'. I pushed the off button and just hoped for the best. I knew we had been on this highway for quite a long time so I figured by the time we got off the highway Jason would be able to help me again.

It had been several hours since we had turned around and neither of us had said a word. I had finally figured out how to reprogram the GPS and now knew exactly how to get home. I looked over at Jason like I had many times over the past couple hours. He still had not moved an inch since he had found out about his dad. My phone's ringing snapped my glance down to its place on the center console. It was my mom. I sighed and picked it up hoping that it was good news.

"Hi, mom."

"You're going to have to postpone your trip back to Harvard for a while."

"Why? What happened?"

"Darien died about a half hour ago."

"No…" I trailed off as I felt tears come to my eyes as I thought about how Jason would react.

"So you two will have to stay for the funeral and such."

"Of course." I hung up the phone and pulled over to the side of the road. This was not something I wanted to tell Jason, but I knew I had to.

"Jason…" He glanced over at me and then around noticing that we were stopped along the side of the road.

"What's wrong?" He asked noticing my tears. He quickly moved his hand to my face to wipe the tears from my face. That action caused me to cry even more. He shouldn't have to go through this. I tried to blink away my tears as he cradled my face in his hands.

"It's about your dad." As I told him, I saw the apprehension in his eyes and facial features.

"He's dead, isn't he?" His voice cracked as he asked the dreaded question. I could only nod before latching onto him as he started to cry. I had never before seen Jason cry, and all I have to say was that I never want to see him cry again. It was the most heart-wrenching thing I have ever experienced. I knew what he was going through having lost my cousin, Sophie's brother six years before. That was the hardest thing I had ever experienced so I could only imagine the pain of

THE NEED TO BELONG

losing ones parent. No matter how unloving and uncaring his dad may have been he was still his father nonetheless. I rubbed small circles on his back as we rocked back and forth. There wasn't really anything that I could say to comfort him so I hoped my actions would suffice. When his sobs finally subsided, I pulled away slowly looking him in his eyes. His eyes were bloodshot and his face was blotchy from all of the crying he had done. I'm sure I looked about the same and was positive my mascara had run. His lips were trembling as he looked at me in such an innocent way that only a small child could muster. Right now he probably did feel like a small child that couldn't control anything that was happening. Everything in his world was tumbling down and he couldn't do anything to stop it from doing so.

Chapter Six

Hey, how are you doing?" I asked Jason after finally finding him sitting in a back room at the funeral home.

"I'm doing ok." I just nodded and sat down beside him on the floor.

"There are a lot of people out there looking for you." I laid my head on his shoulder as he put his arm around me bringing me closer to him.

"Exactly why I'm back here." I nodded and smiled.

"There you two are." My mom walked around the corner throwing her hands up in the air before coming over to us and grabbing both of our arms dragging us back into the viewing area.

"I hate this so much." I rubbed his back with my free hand sympathizing with him. I moved out of the way just in time as one of his aunts crushed him with a hug. I stifled a laugh as he rolled his eyes before she put him at arms length telling him how much he had grown and pinching his cheeks like all aunts and grandmothers seemed to do at these little get together. This really wouldn't count as much of a get together since it was a funeral. Finally, after going through many more aunts and other relatives he was able to come and sit down beside me.

"Break time is it?" He laughed and put his arm around me not saying a word. He didn't need to say anything though. I knew that he was thankful that I was here for him, but why wouldn't I, I'm his best friend and to top it all off his girlfriend. Our parents were of course overjoyed when they found out that we are now a couple. I figured Jason and I would just be put on the back burner since Darien had just died. Nevertheless, no our mothers constantly went on about our future together and just how cute we were together. As I predicted a lot of girls were mad at me because of me dating Jason and it did actually make me a bit happy to see them so jealous.

"When do you two plan on heading back to Harvard?" My mom said as she came up and sat down in a chair next to us.

"Maybe in a couple days after the funeral is over and things die down some." Jason answered for the both of us.

"We already called and explained things to the dean so everything should be in order by the time you get back. We even had a decorator come and get your apartment ready for your arrival." Jason and I just nodded as my mother continued. I laid my head back on Jason's chest listening to his steady heartbeat.

We had sat in that same position until the viewing was over. I didn't even notice that people had came up and talked to Jason while we were sitting there.

"It's time to go." I snapped out of my daze as I felt a rumble in Jason's chest as he spoke to me. I looked up at his smiling face and nodded before getting up slowly with his help.

"I'm famished." Daphne told us while holding her stomach leaning up against a wall.

"Well why don't we all go out to eat because I'm sure we are all famished." I watched as everyone nodded their heads in agreement. Jason chuckled some as he heard my stomach growl. He grabbed my hand as we followed our parents out to the vehicles. Before we got in to leave, we all agreed to go to this posh little Italian restaurant downtown.

"Did you see all the people that came tonight?" I asked Jason trying to make some conversation on the way over to the restaurant.

"It's going to be really hectic tomorrow for the funeral." I just nodded in agreement, as I thought of all the people there was going to have to fit in the funeral home at the same time.

"The funeral home was the largest your mom could find right?" He nodded.

"Only the best for my father." I also nodded as I thought about how true that was.

"My mom wants me to take over the family business as soon as possible."

"What about Harvard?"

"Well once I finish there, but right after I have to take it over."

"So my dad is going to have to keep it under control till you get done with medical school."

"Yeah, but I think my mom is going to hire someone to help your dad out." I nodded as we pulled into the restaurant. The rest of the evening was filled with plans for the business and Jason's and my future. Yes, Jason and I now apparently had a future together. Jason and I had just started dating and our mother's were already planning our wedding. While I listened to both of our mothers, plan our wedding Jason had to listen to my father's business plans. As we exited the restaurant, I leaned up against Jason letting out a long sigh. He chuckled and put his arm around me before kissing me on the top of my head. On the way home, Jason and I didn't say a word, but enjoyed the peace and quiet. This was the first time all day that we hadn't had to endure someone planning our future so we were enjoying every second of it.

"I'll pick you up tomorrow morning." He told me as we pulled up in front of my house. I nodded but just sat there trying to enjoy my time with him. He took my hand in his and rubbed it softly with his thumb. I glanced up at him as he pushed a piece of my hair behind my ear. I smiled before leaning in to kiss him. The kiss was a slow sensual kiss that I thought would never end. It only lasted for a few seconds but to me it felt like a lifetime. We pulled apart only so much that our foreheads were still touching. I raised my hand and caressed his face as he did the same with his other free hand.

"I love you." I felt a jolt in my stomach as I heard those three fatal words that every girl wanted to hear. He chuckled before kissing me on the lips once more. I closed my eyes in contentment and drifted off into what I thought had to be heaven on earth.

"I love you too." I finally managed to say as we parted once more. I felt him smile as his lips met mine in another kiss. I heard my parents pull up into the driveway so I sighed and pulled away from him.

"Goodnight." I said quietly as I got out of the vehicle and headed up to my house. I glanced back to see him wave and pull away from the curb. When I entered the house, I ran up as fast as I could to my room. When I got there, I shut the door and slid down it letting out a long sigh of contentment. He had told me he loved me and I had returned his love. I bit my bottom lip before rubbing my thumb over it softly as the feeling of his kisses hadn't left me yet. I didn't think they would ever leave me and that was fine by me. I got up, danced over to my closet, and changed into my pajamas before dancing over to my bed and falling back onto it. I let out a small giggle and squeal of happiness. Was it too early for Jason and me to tell each other that we loved each other? I didn't think it was, because we have loved each other our entire life so it was easy to love each other in a more romantic way. With that thought, I rolled over under my covers and drifted off into sleep.

The next morning I was woken up by a loud annoying beeping sound. I groaned and rolled over hitting the off button on my alarm clock before sitting up and rubbing the sleep out of my eyes. I glanced at the clock and saw I only had a couple hours before I had to be at the funeral. I walked over to my bathroom and took a quick shower before drying and curling my hair. I then got out a black, knee length, summer dress with matching heels and shawl. I laid them out on my bed slipping on a robe and heading downstairs to grab something from the kitchen. No one was downstairs so I grabbed some orange juice and headed back upstairs to my room. I then proceeded to finish my orange juice while surfing the net to pass the time. I looked up the bookstore in Colorado and the directions on how to get there. I glanced at the clock at the bottom of the screen and quickly pushed print before slipping into my dress.

"Are you ready?" I heard my mother say from the other side of the door. I answered saying, almost, before slipping on my heels and grabbing my shawl and purse. I opened my door and looked down the hall to see my mother and father walking down the hallway at a leisurely pace. I gently closed my door before walking down the hallway with my heels clicking against the floor. As I reached the atrium, my parents were heading out the door toward the car. I stood at the door and waved to my parents as they pulled away from the curb. As soon as they had pulled away, Jason pulled up and I ran toward his car. He got out and opened my door for me also closing it behind me before going over to his side and getting in. He pulled me in for a sweet kiss before pulling away from the curb and making our way to the funeral home. When we entered the funeral home Jason and his mother was pulled into an office to discuss some last minute things with the funeral director and our pastor. I sat in one of the comfortable chairs at the front and waiting on Jason to emerge. My parents walked around the room looking at the flowers that friends and family had sent. I felt someone's hand on my shoulder and I turned around to see Jason staring at the casket in front of us. I gently placed my hand on his and rubbed it affectionately. He then looked down at me and tried to smile but couldn't. I stood up and wrapped my arms around him rubbing small circles on his back as he started to cry. I really didn't know what to say to him I mean who actually knows what to say to someone who just lost their father, so I just opted for holding him and letting him cry. Jason wasn't as strong as he thought himself to be, but to me he was the strongest person in the world. For him to have just lost his father and not be a complete wreck was amazing to me. I know there are different ways of grieving but I knew that he may be calm and collected on the outside but inside he was the wreck I expected him to be. I loved him so much for trying to be strong for his family, but I loved him even more for crying over his father. I heard someone come up behind and then I felt them place a hand on my back.

"Everyone will be arriving soon." I just nodded as I heard my father's voice. I slowly pulled away from Jason and looked him in his bloodshot eyes. I tried to wipe all the evidence of his tears away but it didn't help very much. I sat back down in my chair and pulled him into the chair next to me. Daphne had requested that my family sit up front with their immediate family. She had also requested that we ride with her and Jason in the limo to the cemetery where they would bury him. A few minutes after Jason and I had sat down his grandparents and some of his other family came. After that, every few minutes' people poured in and took their seats getting ready for the service to begin. A few of our friends came and sat behind us for comfort. While Jason talked with Brad and Ben, I talked to Allison and Elizabeth. Apparently, Allison's views had changed some since the last time I had talked to her. Her parents had told her that she couldn't become a psychologist as if she wanted and had to become a respectful businesswoman and join her father in his business. She obviously became upset so now she is rebelling against her parents in every way possible. I laughed along with Elizabeth at the things she had told me she had done. Elizabeth was going to now be home schooled after her parents had a disagreement with her headmaster. Brad and Ben were going to both graduate early and go to Ohio State. Brad wanted to play football there while trying to get his degree in pharmaceuticals. While Ben was going to Morehead State University in Kentucky to get a degree in physical therapy. Their parents weren't as strict as the rest of our parents, which they were extremely grateful. Even though they weren't going to a prestigious school as we were, they were still going into some sort of medical field. Elizabeth's parents planned for her to go to Harvard Law School and join her parents in their firm. It was amazing to me how a summer could change our entire lives. The only person I had talked to the entire summer was Jason so it was understandable that I knew so little about what had happened to everyone. Our pastor, Pastor Sun, went up to the podium to start the service so everyone quieted down and pulled their attention to the front of the room. I grabbed Jason's hand as our pastor began to speak.

"Today is a grievous day for each and every person sitting in this room. Today is the day that we lay to rest Darien Tyler Perry. The way that we had to loose him was most unfortunate and unexpected. He was a loving husband, father, and friend to many. He was the type of person who always tried to help others before he helped himself. He was an esteemed doctor in this community who has helped each of us in our time of need. He will be missed by many but I know for a fact that none of us will ever forget him or the great things he's done for all of us." I could see the sadness in Jason's eyes as he reached out and grabbed his mother's hand as she started to weep. I glanced over at my parents to see my mother also weeping in my father's arms, and I saw tears sliding down my father's face. I had never seen my parents show any emotion like this before. It made them actually seem human. I felt a tear slide down my cheek as I imagined what I would do if I lost my father. Even though I didn't really get along with my parents, I still loved them and they were my parents. I then knew how horribly Jason had to feel at this exact moment. I grasped his hand tighter and rubbed his hand with my other hand. I saw him glance down at our hands and smile slightly before bringing my hands up to his lips and kissing them gently. I smiled back at him before laying my head on his shoulder. Daphne then proceeded to get up and talk about Darien and some of the memories they had together.

"Darien was a wonderful husband. He always went out of his way to make sure I had exactly what I wanted and needed. I remember the first time I ever saw him and at that moment, I knew that was the man I wanted to marry. I was at my senior prom and I saw him across the room with another girl, and I decided I was going to do anything to get that man. So, I did just that, I went over and took him away from that girl, and he didn't leave my side after that. He was always a wonderful father to our Jason and always knew what to do when I had no clue what to do. I'm going to miss him and everything about him that made me who I am." While talking Daphne started to cry so, my mother went up to comfort her as my father took over sharing memories about Darien. Before it was all over, everyone had shed tears or laughed at a shared memory of Darien. Pastor Sun ended the service with a prayer and invited everyone to the graveside services. Jason and Daphne stood up and hugged everyone who proceeded by them before heading to their cars. I glanced out the window as I stood by waiting for everyone to give their condolences and saw that it was raining. I sighed as my smallest bit of happiness left me. Rainy days always seemed to damper my mood instantaneously, and so this day was officially one of the worst days ever in my book. I always wondered why the weather always seemed to be unbearable during a funeral. I glanced over at Jason and noticed he had a break as his grandmother was now holding onto Daphne and didn't seem to want to let go anytime soon. I gently hit my hand against his before nodding toward the window. He rolled his eyes and sighed putting his arm around me bringing me closer to him and kissing the top of my head.

"I didn't think it could get any worse." Right as those words left his lips it started to thunder. I glared at him and elbowed him in the ribs; he sent me an apologetic look before smiling down at me.

"So are you going to be snuggling with me under my umbrella or are you going to insist on having your own?"

"I wouldn't dare pass up a chance of snuggling with my boyfriend."

"You two need to stop. This is Darien's funeral, and you should be ashamed of yourselves." I heard my mother's accusing voice in my ear. Jason heard her and sighed before rubbing his hand up and down my side.

"That's everyone so ladies please go to the limo out front and will the pallbearers please step forward." The funeral director led Daphne, my mom, and I out to the limo. The limo driver stood with the door open to the limo waiting for us to enter the limo. We stood outside the limo and waited until the pallbearers had placed Darien in the hearse and headed toward their vehicles. Right after I sat down in the limo Jason sat down beside me and my dad beside my mom. The limo door closed and the engine started. Jason put his arm around me and I leaned into him as we waited for the funeral precession to start. By the time, we reached the cemetery Jason and I had drifted in and out of sleep several times. The limo door opened and Daphne stepped out under an umbrella, my mom and dad following the process. Jason then stepped out and helped me out of the limo. Jason took the umbrella held over our head from the driver and handed it to me. He kissed me on the cheek and ran over to where the hearse was along with my father. Daphne, my mother, and I then headed over to the where a tent was set up for the graveside services to take place. Daphne sat down in one of the chairs set out for the family. Darien's parents had passed away and he was an only child so his only immediate family was Daphne and Jason. There were three other seats beside the two for Daphne and Jason whom I assumed was for my parents and me. Daphne had made sure that my parents and I were treated just like immediate family during this entire ordeal. I saw my mom sit down beside Daphne so I sat down on the other side of her a seat away so that Jason could sit by his mother. I glanced over to where Jason was carrying his father's coffin toward us. He glanced up at me and I smiled gently at him as his face was set in stone. I knew he was trying to be strong and I was so proud of him being so strong in a time like this. Finally, the coffin was set down before us and Jason took his seat beside me. I glanced behind us and saw the cemetery scattered with black umbrellas heading toward us. I felt Jason's wet hands grasp mine as he stared straight ahead at the coffin. I stifled a giggle as I took him in. He looked like a soaking wet golden retriever. He glanced toward me and I pushed his wet hair out of his face and giggled again.

"What is so funny?" He stifled a smile as I wiped the drops of water off his nose.

"You look like a wet dog." That got him to smile as he leaned forward kissing me softly as he pushed my hair out of my eyes.

"And you my darling look beautiful."

"Now you're just trying to make me feel bad." He chuckled before wrapping his free arm around me and bringing me closer. I felt the water from his suit seep through my dress, but I didn't really care even though from his grin I knew he was doing it on purpose. All during the graveside service, I stared at the graves in the distance and the rain pouring down on them. Soon after we were all gone there would be a grave just like those others for Darien. I would probably never come to see the grave like most of the people here, but I didn't really think it mattered. After all, it wasn't as if he actually knew that I was there. I felt Jason pat me on my leg as he got up with his mother and my parents to get a rose off the coffin. I snapped myself out of my daze and got up along with them carefully removing a red rose from the coffin. When I got home, I would put the rose in a box full of sand to preserve it. I looked up from where I was standing and saw a mass of black umbrellas heading back toward their cars. I felt Jason pull me under his umbrella as we started to walk back to the limo. After this, we were to head to our church where we would have a dinner for all of Darien's friends and family. On the way to our church, everyone in the limo was talking adamantly about the funeral and some of the encounters they had with the people that had come. Jason and I sat quietly reminiscing about the days events while they continued to chat.

"What about our cars?" I asked Jason as the limo pulled away from the church's recreation center.

"They're going to drop them off here." I nodded before he pulled me into the recreation center, which was already full of people.

"Do you want me to go find us a table?" I asked when I noticed Ben and Brad coming toward us.

"No, stay with me." I looked up at his face as he rubbed small circles on my palm. I just nodded not wanting to go against any of his wishes today. I didn't know what I was getting myself into as I stood with Jason while he talked with Brad and Ben. I used to be best friends with the two but over the past couple years we drifted apart so I wasn't so sure we'd still have very much in common. Of course, I was proven wrong when I realized we still and a lot in common. Also, my interacting with Jason's friends seemed to lift his moods some. I guess he was afraid of the same thing I was, his friends and I not getting along.

"Do you think you'll like Harvard?" Ben decided to ask us.

"No." I muttered but I felt Jason squeeze my hand and decided to change my answer as Ben had a confused look on his face.

"I mean I'm sure it will be wonderful considering how prestigious it is made out to be. Besides we have our own apartments off campus that our mother's just had professionally decorated." I hoped that neither of the two would see through my facade. Maybe they would assume that I had changed just as we had grown apart over the years. I saw Ben smile and he started to go on about all the good things he had heard about Harvard. I glanced over at Brad to see if he had bought it, he had been my best friend in the entire world and used to be able to read me quite well, his eyes were narrowed at me as if he was trying to see through all the barriers I had been putting up. We made eye contact and I knew that he knew I was lying.

"I have to go use the restroom I'll be right back." I turned and walked away from the group picking up my pace once I thought I had made it out of eyeshot. I walked quickly into the first room I came upon and closed the door behind me. No sooner had I closed it the door opened once again. I spun around to see Brad come in and close the door. I sighed and sat down on one of the chairs that surrounded the round table in the middle of the room.

"What's going on Claire?" I knew I couldn't lie to Brad so I motioned for him to sit down in one of the free chairs.

"Tell me what you know." I knew he knew some things so I needed to know what to tell him and what not to tell him.

"I know that you don't want to go to Harvard, I know you searched for Sophie all summer, I know you know something about her whereabouts that no one else knows, and I think you are going to go after her." Wow, he really could read me well or someone had told him all of this.

"No, I just know you that well, and Jason had hinted something about Sophie." I laughed as he answered my unspoken response.

"I'm not going to go back to Harvard when I leave here in a couple days."

"Does Jason know that?"

"He might have guessed that, but I haven't told him."

"You have to be honest with him or what happened with us will happen again but with you two." Of course, Brad would bring up the fact that we had dated in my sophomore year for about eleven months.

"I'm sorry."

"Stop apologizing we were both young and stupid. You have nothing to be sorry about." I nodded and smiled as I realized how good I felt to actually be on speaking terms with him again.

"Thanks. I think I needed to hear that."

"Well I'm sorry I never told you."

"Do you think I'm making the right decision?"

"Which one?"

"What do you mean?"

"The going after Sophie, not going to Harvard, not telling Jason, loving Jason. Your choice really."

"I hate how you know me so well."

"Someone has to do it."

"Well?"

"Oh, so you want me to answer all of them."

"Duh."

"Well I think going after Sophie is a good choice. I know you never wanted to go to Harvard, but I want you to be able to fulfill your dreams too. You really need to tell Jason or well you know what will happen. As for falling in love with him, I don't think that there is anything I could tell you to help you with that except that you should just follow your heart."

"You're actually smart for a guy." I laughed pushing his shoulder playfully.

"Well I don't know how a blonde like you got into Harvard."

"Don't stereotype me Brad. I have a 4.0 GPA thank you very much."

"I say you cheated your way through." He laughed as I playfully smacked him as if I was actually offended.

"There you two are. They are getting ready to say the prayer." We both looked up as Jason stood in the doorway his face unreadable.

"Thanks dude." Brad said getting up and slapping Jason on the back as he left the room.

"He knows." I stood up and made my way over to him at the door.

"I don't care just come on." I tried to make eye contact with him but it seemed impossible to do as he turned to walk out the door.

"What's wrong?" I grabbed his arm and forced him to turn and look at me.

"My problem is that you would choose to talk to your ex rather than talk to your current boyfriend."

"Are you jealous?"

"I think I just made that very clear."

"Well there is no reason to be. He just recognized that there wasn't something I wasn't telling and wanted to talk to me about it."

"He could have just asked me instead of seeking you out to do so."

"I was the one lying Jason not you."

"I'm not comfortable with you being alone with him."

"Why? Do you not trust me?"

"It's not you I don't trust."

"What is that supposed to mean?"

"Figure it out since you claim to be so smart." I stood in shock as he turned and walked down the hall toward the double doors at the end leading to the dining area.

"Claire what just happened?" I turned to see Allison and Elizabeth standing a couple doors down at the bathroom.

"He's jealous because I was talking to Brad."

"We heard that part Claire. We mean the other part." Allison asked with a scrutinizing stare.

51

"What is with everyone putting another meaning behind every question they ask me?" I slid down the doorframe to the ground putting my head on my knees.

"Do you really know where Sophie is?" Elizabeth was able to ask before Allison elbowed her in the ribs.

"How did you know that?"

"Thin walls." I rolled my eyes, sighing, before nodding.

"So does she know you're coming?"

"No, and no one else knows, so you two are not to say a word of this." They both nodded and pretended to zip and lock their lips before throwing away the key.

"How did you find her?" We all froze as someone opened the double doors and headed toward the bathroom.

"I can't talk about it here, someone might hear."

"We're talking later Claire." I nodded before they offered me their hands, helping me to my feet. We then walked out into the dining area just in time to hear the prayer and get in line for the buffet.

Chapter Seven

All during the dinner, no one at my table said a word. I glanced around uncomfortably as Jason glared at Brad, who was staring at me. Allison and Elizabeth kept giving each other furtive glances while Ben sat there opening and closing his mouth debating whether to say anything. Evidently, I had gone off into my own thoughts again because when I looked up Allison and Elizabeth were sitting across from me tapping their fingers on the table simultaneously. I looked to my side and saw we were the only ones left at our table.

"Where are the boys?"

"They went to talk." Allison told me as she inspected her nails.

"Where?" I asked panicky as I quickly got up from the table.

"That doesn't matter." Elizabeth told me flanking my right side as Allison flanked my left grabbing a hold of my arms.

"What does matter is that we need to talk and them talking makes this the perfect opportunity to talk about what we need to talk about." I raised my eyebrows in confusion but then she nodded to the table behind us, which had all of our parents sitting around it. I opened my mouth in understanding and nodded before following them to the classroom we were at before. I walked in and sat down in one of the chairs with Elizabeth as Allison closed and locked the door behind us.

"Talk." Allison commanded once she had sat down at the table.

"Thin walls." I reminded her smirking.

"Talk quietly and quickly then." Elizabeth said, her smirk matching mine.

"I see you have improved your smirking skills since I left."

"Yeah I know isn't it great?"

"Shut up! Both of you, and start talking." I looked at Elizabeth with an amused look.

"You know what I mean." Allison sighed before starting to rub her temples with her fingers.

"Ok, well after Jason and I stopped looking for Sophie I found a blank book in my desk with a letter from Sophie. This made me think that she had been planning on running away for a while."

"Did she tell you that in the letter?" Elizabeth said in a hushed tone.

"No, but she talked about how she might not always be there with me in reality, and then before she disappeared we were talking about me leaving and she mentioned several times that she didn't want me to leave, and she had that look in her eye that I didn't recognize till now. She was going to do anything to come with me."

"Something wasn't right for her to want to leave like that."

"Well I wanted to leave because my parents were controlling my future and not letting me have a choice."

"I think there's more than that." I looked at Elizabeth in a perplexed way. "What do you mean?"

"Do you know something we don't?" Allison asked right after.

"Kind of." Elizabeth mumbled not daring to look either of us in the eye.

"What is 'kind of' supposed to mean?" I said turning her chair toward me so she had no choice but to look at me.

"She might have mentioned something about how things weren't so good at home."

"What?" Allison asked shocked as I just sighed and leaned back in my chair.

"My family isn't the nicest people in the world. Actually my parents are the nice ones in the family."

"Are you serious?" I nodded before getting up and pacing around the room.

"Well you know about what happened to her brother Hayden right?"

"Yeah I know he died when he was like sixteen in a car crash."

"Well her parents and two older sisters never let her live it down and I think they blame his death on her."

"She was only like eight when it happened, and it wasn't as if she was driving."

"He was going to be their famous doctor and everything. They considered him to be the perfect son, but I think they put too much stress on him just like they did with Sophie."

"Weren't you two close?"

"Yeah, but I didn't get blamed Sophie did."

"But she had nothing to do with it."

"I know but that's not the point. She was the only one with him besides me at the time and they had to blame it on someone, and my parents made sure they didn't blame it on me. I think she blames herself some too."

"That's horrible."

"Anyway they are always telling her that she needs to make her brother proud and that she has to live up to him. They are always comparing her to him. I think the stress got to her and she just finally had enough and decided to leave."

"Do you blame yourself like Sophie does?"

"No, a drunk driver hit us there was nothing that any of us could have done especially Sophie."

"Well, where is she?"

"I think she's in Colorado."

"Why do you say that?" Allison asked as soon as I had sat back down.

"Shortly after I stopped looking for her, someone called me from a Colorado area code. The person only said word and it was Claire. The person sounded exactly like Sophie."

"It could have been anyone." Elizabeth reasoned.

"I thought that too till I called the number back and it was a bookstore."

"So? I know Sophie wanted to open a bookstore." Elizabeth said as Allison sat there trying to take it all in.

"Well the bookstore's name was Laugh Bookstore."

"What's that have to do with anything?" Allison finally said.

"Everything." I grabbed my purse from the table and pulled out the letter and the map. I glanced at the map and my eyes widened as I glanced back over at the letter before handing them over to the girls.

"This is the letter she sent you." I nodded as the read it over.

"Do you notice how she signs?"

"Yeah, Love Always Unconditionally Forever in Hope."

"It took me a while but I finally figure it out. If you take the first letter of each word, it spells LAUFH."

"But that's not Laugh."

"Yeah I know. That's why I looked up the bookstore on the internet. Its spelled L-A-U-F-H. I thought it was just a typo when I first saw it, but now I get it." Allison and Elizabeth's eyes widened as they realized too where Sophie was.

"So she's in Colorado and she opened a bookstore and she is leaving you clues so you can find her." I nodded as we sat in stunned silence for a while.

"Have you told anyone besides us?"

"No, no one."

"Jason is going to be even more upset Claire."

"I'm going to be more upset about what?" I slowly turned around as I head Jason's voice from the door.

"What happened to you?" Allison said standing up beside me.

"What did you do?" I gasped as I saw his face was covered with blood.

"You're not going to go anywhere near him any more."

"What are you talking about?"

"I don't want you anywhere near Brad ever again."

"Why?"

"Stop asking stupid questions and listen to me."

"It's not a stupid question. I want to know why I'm supposed to stay away from one of my best friends."

"Because I don't want you to."

"That's not a good enough reason. You're just being possessive and jealous."

"So what if I am. It's for a good reason."

"What is that reason?"

"You don't need to know!" I stepped away from him as he screamed in my face. I saw Allison and Elizabeth sneak out the door behind him out of the corner of my eye.

"Yes, I do." I tried to stand my ground but it was hard considering how weak I felt when he towered over me.

"Do you care about him?"

"Of course I care about him."

"Fine. He can take you back to Harvard or wherever you plan on going."

"What?!" I grabbed his arm as he started to walk out the door. He jerked his arm from my grasp and walked out the door anyway.

"Claire!" Elizabeth ran into the room grabbing my arm and dragging me out the door, down the hall, and outside. Once outside I saw Allison and Ben standing over Brad, who was lying on the ground in a heap. I picked up my pace and ran over to where he was laying.

"What happened?" I asked Ben as I knelt down at Brad's side.

"Jason told him he wanted to talk so they went outside and I followed. When I got out here, they were yelling at each other and then Jason punched him. I tried to separate them but it was no use." I glared at Allison and Elizabeth for not letting me go see where they were, before I ran my hand through Brad's hair slowly trying to wake him up.

"Brad are you ok?" He groaned and held onto his stomach as he woke up.

"Yeah, I think he just broke one of my ribs and maybe my nose." He laughed uneasily before grabbing his ribs in pain.

"We're taking you to the hospital." Allison told him as Ben and I helped him up and to the car, which we all pilled in.

"Where's Jason?"

"He's inside probably trying to clean himself up."

"You should have gone with him."

"He didn't want me to."

56

"What were you two fighting about?" Elizabeth asked from the front seat of the Ben's Hummer.

"He didn't want me around Claire; because he thinks I'm still in love with her and is afraid I'm going to try to steal her from him."

"I can't believe he would even think something like that." I said in disbelief. Ben who was looking back at us turned back toward the road quickly and Brad turned away from me.

"Do you still love me?" I turned away from him and looked out the window once I saw him nod. Brad and I were each other's first love but I had thought he had moved on after our not so nice breakup. I guess from the looks Allison and Elizabeth were giving me they had thought the same thing. Now that he was bringing up these old feelings, I didn't know what to do. Was it possible for me to love two people at the same time? That was a question that I think I would only be able to answer with time.

"Turn here." I heard Elizabeth tell Ben from the front of the car.

"Are you ok?" I glanced over at Brad who was staring at me with a caring expression.

"I should be asking you that question. I'm not the one with the broken rib and nose."

"You know exactly what I was referring."

"I know, but I'm not ready to talk about it yet." He nodded slowly before looking back out the window.

"Allison, Claire, help him into the waiting room and we'll find a place to park." We nodded and helped Brad out of the Hummer and into the waiting room. We sat him down in one of the chairs before we went up to the front desk and told them what had happened.

"You're in luck he won't have to wait any, so a nurse will be right down to take him up." I nodded and went over and sat down beside Brad and Allison. As soon as I had sat down Ben and Elizabeth walked in joining us. Before we knew it, a nurse had come to take Brad up to get examined.

"I wonder how long we'll actually be here." I just shrugged as Elizabeth flicked through the channels on the TV and Allison looked through some of the magazines lying around.

We sat in the waiting room for about two hours before a doctor came down and told us that he had broken a few of his ribs and did in fact have a broken nose. They were going to bandage him up and give him some painkillers before sending him home. We waited for another hour before Brad finally emerged into the waiting room, and we could take him home.

"Ready to go?" We all gathered our stuff together and headed out the door that Brad was already walking through.

"How are you feeling?" I asked him once I had caught up with him.

"I feel great, but I want to know how you're feeling."

"I'm fine Brad." I looked away from him to avoid his doubting stare.

"You always were bad at hiding things from me." I laughed nervously before looking over at him again.

"Yeah. How do you expect me to react when I find out my ex-boyfriend is still in love with me and gets into a fight with my current boyfriend over me?"

"I don't know. I just want to know if you still feel something, anything, for me."

"I can't answer that Brad and you know that."

"No, it's not that you can't. It's that you won't. You're afraid Claire and I get that, but don't stand here and tell me you don't still have feelings for me when I know that you do." I looked at his hand, which was currently holding onto my arm, stopping me from walking any further toward the car. I then looked up at him with pleading eyes.

"Don't make me do this right now."

"Fine we won't, but we're going to have to eventually." I nodded and walked away from him as soon as he had released my arm.

"So girls you want me to take you back to the church so you can get your cars?" Ben asked as soon as we were all in the car.

"My ride home was Jason." I told them quietly after the girls had agreed for him to take them back to the church.

"Then we'll take you home after we drop the girls off." I smiled and thanked them as he pulled out of the hospital parking lot onto the highway. It only took ten minutes to get back to the church, but it was a very long and quiet ten minutes. I seemed to have a lot of those quiet awkward moments lately. Ben pulled into the parking lot and there were three cars left. I recognized the one immediately as Jason's car.

"I forgot something inside." I told Brad and Ben before going into the church.

"Jason." I called as soon as I had closed the door behind me. As I was walking down the hall looking for him I realized I had actually forgotten my purse, so at least coming in here wasn't in vain. I went to the room that the girls and I were talking in earlier today and found my purse sitting on the table. I grabbed it off the table and went to walk out the door when I heard someone cough. I turned around and walked toward where I thought it had come from. I found Jason sitting on the floor his head in his hands.

"Jason?" He looked up and I saw that he had been crying. I knelt down beside him placing my hand on his face wiping away all the evidence of the tears that he had cried.

"What are you doing here?"

"I just got back from the hospital and I saw your car was here so I decided to come look for you."

"Did you leave Brad then?" I couldn't help but laugh some at how pathetic he was actually being.

"I was never with Brad to actually have a chance to leave him." Jason scoffed and got up and started to walk away from me.

"Stop being a jealous idiot and get over yourself." I called out to him. He stopped and turned slowly toward me.

"I have every reason to be jealous. You left me for my best friend, your ex-boyfriend."

"I didn't leave you. He was hurt and needed my help. Do I need to remind you that he is my friend too?"

"He's not my friend."

"Stop being so childish! Just because he still has feelings for me doesn't mean you need to ruin your friendship with him."

"You never said whether or not you still have feelings for him."

"Don't change the subject."

"I'm not changing the subject. You are just avoiding it." I stared at him knowing that there was no way I was going to be able to put this off anymore.

"I don't know."

"What don't you know?" His eyes narrowed trying to figure out what I was trying to say.

"I don't know if I still have feelings for him or not."

"So this has all been a lie?"

"What? No! I love you Jason! I just don't know if I still love Brad."

"I can't believe you! We're over!" I started to run after him as he walked out of the door, but I stopped as I realized what had just happened. I dropped to my knees as my body was overcome with my sobs. I felt a hand on my back start rubbing small circles so I latched onto them and burying my head on his chest as he wrapped his arms around me.

"I love you Claire. " I looked up at the face of my savior and smiled through my tears.

Chapter Eight

I love you too, Brad." I sat in sheer shock at what had just come out of my mouth and by the way, Brad was staring at me, I could tell he was experiencing the same thing.

"Do you really mean that?" He finally was able to say.

"I don't know. I mean I said it so I must have been thinking it, but I can't have meant it because I love Jason."

"You can love more than one person Claire." He tried to explain lifting my face up to look at him.

"I don't want to do this right now. Jason just dumped me, and I'm not thinking clearly. See that's what happened, I wasn't thinking clearly." I smiled happily, as I had finally figured out what had happened.

"Are you sure about that?" Doubt filled my mind once more as he said that.

"Stop confusing me." I told him as I scrambled to my feet and tried to walk toward the door, but he grabbed me pulling me back toward him.

"No. You're going to tell me how you really feel about me right now."

"I don't know! Is that what you wanted to hear?"

"No! I want to know if you still love me like I still love you."

"Well sorry to burst your bubble but I don't know!" I pulled myself out of his grasp, ran out of the church, and kept running. I didn't stop until I was five blocks away and I fell to the ground in pain and exhaustion. I pulled off my heels and threw them a few feet away from me, as they were the things causing me so much pain. I knew that they weren't the only reason why I was in pain though. My heart was broken into a million pieces and my head was killing me from all of the stress and the drama of the day. I massaged my feet gently trying to ease the pain. I decided that I might as well keep walking considering my house was only a couple more blocks away. I got up, limped over to my heels, and picked them up from where I had discarded them. I then started to walk the rest of the way to my house. As soon as I was able to see my house, I mustered up enough energy and ran the rest of the way. Once inside my house I collapsed to the ground. I looked down at my feet and saw they were covered with blood and dirt. I crawled toward the steps and tried to make my way up to my room. It must have taken a half hour or more just to make it to my room. I then crawled toward my shower and got in turning the water on hot. I used the bars to pull myself up to a standing position. I then stripped off my dress and threw it out of the shower on the floor along with the rest of my clothes I had on. I washed away all of the dirt, blood, tears, and grime I had managed to accumulate from the day. My feet burned as the water hit the open wounds. I turned off the water, grabbed my robe, and stepped out of the shower. I put my hair up in a towel, walked over to my vanity, and sat down. I opened a drawer and grabbed a medicine bag out. I got out the anti-bacterial and Band-Aids and started to patch up my feet the best I could. I then cleaned all the make-up that was left on my face off and started to pick up everything I had thrown on the floor. I threw all my dirty clothes in the hamper, went over to my purse, and tried to put all of the contents that had fallen out back in. I picked up my phone and noticed that I had a voicemail. I sighed and debated whether to listen to it. After much debate, I decided to listen to it.

"Claire, I miss you and I love you. Please don't try to find me and take me home. I'm happy here." I saved the message to my phone memory and leaned against the wall. That message was from Sophie and she was actually happy where she was. She was actually better off than I was at this moment.

"I can't stay here anymore." I told myself as I got up grabbing a duffel bag and started throwing stuff I would need in it. I put all the money I had saved up in my purse and put a blanket, some extra clothes, my laptop, and everything else that was of some importance to me. I quickly changed into my most comfortable jeans, a T-shirt, my favorite hoodie, and some comfortable sneakers. I grabbed my duffel bag, and my purse that I had brought on the trip with Jason, and walked out of my room. I glanced back at it one more time and a sole tear fell down my cheek before I ran downstairs and out to the garage. I grabbed the closest keys to the door, which was my mom's brand new yellow and black Camaro. I threw my stuff in the back seat and got in starting it up. I pulled out of the driveway and sped off down the road not looking back once.

Before I knew it, I had made it out of Charleston and I was making my way across the West Virginia border into Kentucky. I got out the map I had made off and figured out that I needed to take I-64 W all the way to Kansas. For the next 504 miles I would be on the highway, so I decided I needed to stop at the next gas station fill up the Camaro and get some necessities I would need for the next eight hours and forty some minutes. I found a gas station in no time and pulled in and up to the pumps. I got out and started to fill it up. I leaned up against the side of the car and sighed before looking around at the small town. I heard the click signaling that it was done. I then headed inside to pay for the gas and get some food and drinks for the journey ahead.

"Is that all for you?" I nodded and handed the man, who must have been only a couple years older than I, the money. I glanced down and saw his nametag read 'Casey'.

"Thanks." I turned around and ran right into a guy that had just walked in. I looked up at him to see a gorgeous guy staring back at me. He had light brown hair that fell in his face, which he pushed out of the way so I could then see his blue eyes with specks of silver. He was definitely a musician I could tell that much by his clothes and the way he stood.

"I'm so sorry." I apologized trying to pick up the bags I had dropped when I ran into him.

"Could you move?" I glanced up at him to see him shake his head and laugh before walking around me to the counter. Figures someone as gorgeous as him would be a jerk.

"Whatever." I picked up my bags and walked out of the gas station to my car. I threw the bags in the back seat before getting in and starting up my car. I went to pull out of my parking space when I had to slam on my breaks to not hit the '67 Impala that sped by me loudly honking the horn. I noticed that it was the same guy that I had run into in the store.

"Jerk." I mumbled before pulling out and heading back onto the highway. Once I had got back with the flow of the traffic, I set my cruise control and turned on the radio starting to relax. I had left my home and everything I had known to go on a wild goose chase for Sophie, who was supposedly happy. I sighed looking out at the scenery that was passing by me.

I had never been on a road trip by myself before, and now I realized why. I was bored out of my mind and there was nothing I could do about it. I had already tried to play every road game imaginable, but it seemed pointless and stupid with no one else with me. It was starting to get dark so I really needed to focus on the road now more than before. This was the first time I had ever driven by myself for a long distance at night, so there wasn't going to be any extra eyes to help me out when I needed them. I turned on my headlights and noticed that the traffic was starting to get thinner around me. The traffic dying down was at least somewhat helpful for me. The truck in front of me had a bed full of scrap metal, so I tried to keep my distance from him not wanting to have something fly out and hit me. No sooner had I thought that, a piece of metal flew out and I had to swerve to miss it, but I still felt something hit under my car. I slowed down a bit incase something was going to happen, but nothing did so I decided to pass the truck so I would have less to worry about. I glanced at my rearview mirror and noticed him pulling off onto the exit ramp. I glanced at my map and noticed that it was the last exit ramp for a while so it wasn't a surprise when most of the people around me had pulled off as well. I didn't want to waste the money I did have, on a staying at a hotel when I could just pull over and sleep in my car if need be. I heard a beeping sound and glanced down at my gauges to see that I evidently had a leak in my gas tank because my gas gauge was going down quickly. I quickly pulled off to the side of the road and turned off the car immediately. I grabbed my purse and got out of the car. I glanced around and saw no one insight so I pulled my phone out of my purse but I had no signal. I let out a frustrated cry and threw the phone back in the purse. I grabbed a light and looked under the car to see gas pouring out of the gas tank. I heard a rumble and looked up to see headlights heading toward me I quickly ran toward the road and started to wave them down. They slowed down and pulled in behind my car. I groaned when I noticed that it was the same car that had tried to run me over in the parking lot, so that meant it was the same guy I had ran into in the store. He opened his car door and stepped out shaking his head as he walked toward me with a smug look on his face.

"What did you get yourself into now?" I didn't get to respond not that he wanted me to because he then bent over looking under the car shaking his head.

"You really got yourself into a mess didn't you Blondie." He wiped his hands off on his pants and gave me a once over.

"I don't know what happened."

"Well it looks like something hit your gas tank, so you're lucky that your car didn't blow up." My eyes widened as he said this.

"Whoa."

"The car still could blow up you know." He smirked as I jumped away from the car.

"Well what am I supposed to do then?"

"I don't know Blondie." I stood in shock as he strutted away toward his car. I finally snapped out of it and ran after him.

"Can you give me a ride?" He flung open the door on his car and got in before looking up at me smugly.

"I don't have all day Blondie." He nodded his head sharply to the seat next to him. I smiled and thanked him before grabbing my bag out of the car and getting in the passenger side of his car. I winced as the door slammed shut behind me as the wind picked up. I tossed my bag in the backseat but paused as I saw a vintage Fender guitar sitting in the backseat. His voice then snapped me out of my daze.

"Looks like its going to rain Blondie." I rolled my eyes at the use of my new nickname as we pulled away from my car. I turned in my seat and watched my Mom's car as we sped off down the highway. I felt my heart jump in my chest as I heard an explosion and saw a burst of flames in the distance where my Mom's car used to be.

"Now that's something I can't fix Blondie." He chuckled as he glanced in the rear view mirror at the burning car. I turned and glared at him before slumping down in my seat.

"You don't talk much do you Blondie?" I let out a sigh before looking out the window. I was still a little sore about what had happened at the gas station earlier.

"Since you aren't going to talk, I suppose you won't mind if I turn on some music?" He turned toward me with his hand on the dial waiting to see if I was going to object. When I didn't, he turned the knob and 'Highway to Hell' blasted throughout the car.

"Can you turn it down some?" I tried to yell over the music. He turned toward me and smirked before turning the music down.

"So Blondie can talk."

"My name is Claire." He smirked before looking at the road.

"Are you going to tell me your name?" He smirked as he kept his eyes on the road. I had a feeling that he was doing this just to annoy me.

"It's raining." I pointed out after about five minutes of silence.

"And they say blondes are dumb."

"Are you always this insightful?" I snapped before glaring at the road.

"So why are you running away?" I whipped around to look at him.

"How did you know?"

"Well that was obviously your Dad's car and you had luggage with you but not enough to be moving or going to college, and most people your age would have someone with them if they were going on a vacation. Therefore, I opted that you're a spoiled brat who couldn't take it when daddy wouldn't buy you the latest thing so you decided to hack it out in the real world. Am I right?"

"No, not even close." I smirked back at him as he raised an eyebrow.

"Well would you like to enlighten me on what happened to make daddy's little princess run away?"

"I think I liked it better when you called me Blondie."

"Well the only way you're going to get me to call you that again is if you tell me what made you run away."

"Oh joy! My parents wanted me to go to Harvard to be a doctor and I want to be a writer, and my best friend ran away so I'm trying to find her, and then

I had some guy trouble and I couldn't take it anymore, and I got a call from Sophie so now I'm going to go find her." I breathed deeply as I had said that all in one breath. I looked over at him waiting to get a reaction but all he did was turn back toward the road his face unreadable.

"Aren't you going to make some witty comment or something?"

"Nah. Sorry Blondie."

"So I'm back to Blondie. I guess that's a good thing. Are you going to tell me anything about you?"

"No, I don't think I will."

"Come on, I've just basically told you my life story, so the least you could do is tell me your name or where you're headed."

"You didn't tell me where you're going."

"Colorado." I looked at him expectantly as he continued to look at the road.

"Isn't that a coincidence, that's exactly where I'm going."

"Seriously?" He nodded with the same smug look on his face that made me feel like he knew something I didn't.

"So you're looking for your friend Sophie."

"Yeah. Why?"

"Do you know where she's at exactly or what?"

"I think she opened a bookstore called LAUFH Bookstore in Breckenridge, Colorado."

"You think?"

"No, I know she did."

"Oh ok, so how are you planning on getting there?"

"Well I was hoping that maybe since you're going there I might just tag along?"

"I don't know. I'm kind of a loner."

"I noticed, but it would really help me out if you could take me there."

"I guess I could, but there's going to be some rules."

"Really what would those be?" I asked sarcastically.

"No touching the radio, no complaining, you're going to pay for your share of the gas and everything else we may need, and no incessant talking. I might add to these later, but for now that's it."

"Sounds reasonable enough." I told him agreeing to his terms.

"My name is Xander." I smiled as we both turned back to look at the road.

"Nice to meet you Xander." I told him giggling some at the circumstances.

"Yeah, yeah whatever." I couldn't help but smile knowing that I was starting to get to him. My new goal was to breakthrough Xander's tough guy exterior.

"So why are you going to Colorado?" He chuckled and shook his head.

"You really don't give up do you Blondie?" I shook my head and gave him the best puppy dog eyes I could.

"Sorry to tell you this Blondie, but that doesn't work on me, I have a little sister who tries the same thing all the time."

"Aha so you do have a family!"

"You just think you're so great because you got one thing out of me don't you." He actually smiled at me, which made my heart beat wildly. One of the main reasons I was leaving was to get away from guys, so being in a car with a very attractive, smart, and witty guy wasn't helping. Maybe it wasn't guys I was trying to get away from though; maybe it was those two guys in particular.

"What's your sister's name?" I cleared my throat trying to calm my nerves and heart down some.

"Alexia."

"How much younger is she than you?"

"Ten minutes, we're twins."

"She must be gorgeous then." I quickly clamped my hand over my mouth and my eyes went wide as I realized what I had just said.

"I guess I should thank you then." I chanced a glance at him, saw a twinkle in his eye, and knew he wouldn't let me live that down.

"How old are you?" That question had been bugging me since I had first seen him.

"I'm twenty, you?" I guess he wasn't that much older than me.

"I'm eighteen."

"I think you know enough about me now, so let's talk more about you."

"The only thing I found out is that you have a twin sister and you're twenty."

"That's all you need to know. Do you have any brothers or sisters?"

"Nope, I'm an only child."

"I bet you are spoiled."

"If you mean my parents doting me with things then yes, but otherwise no." I glared at him before looking out at the vast darkness surrounding us.

"I bet your boyfriend is worried sick about you."

Chapter Nine

I don't have a boyfriend anymore." I told him in an icy tone.
"Bad break up?"
"You could say that." I saw him smile out of the corner of my eye and look back out at the road.

"So what happened, or is it too early to talk about it?"

"No, it's fine. He got mad because I was talking to my ex-boyfriend, his best friend. Then they got in a fight because my ex-boyfriend still liked me."

"Now that is quite the break up story." He chuckled shaking his head.

"Don't you have a girlfriend back home, wherever that may be, that is missing you?"

"Nah. I'm not the type of guy that has a girlfriend." The smile that was on my face faded when I heard him say that

"Oh really. Why's that?"

"Never really was fond of some girl bossing me around all the time."

"What if you found someone that wasn't like that?"

"Subtle, but I don't know how well it would work out between us Blondie."

"That's not what I meant!" I practically yelled which got a hearty laugh out of him.

"Sure Blondie." I glared at him as he smiled brightly at me.

"Will you just shut up and drive?"

"What? You were the one that wanted to talk."

"Fine, no more talking." His eyes danced with the laughter he was trying so hard to hold in. We continued to sit in silence for about five minutes before he started humming. At first, the humming was quite a pleasant relief from the silence, but then it started to get annoying as he got louder and began to start singing loudly. It wasn't that he was a bad singer because he had an amazing voice, but he then started to alternate between playing an air guitar and drumming on his steering wheel. I hid my smile as I watched him continue to let loose.

"You're a really talented air guitarist." I finally managed to tell him while keeping a straight face.

"Actually I'm a really talented guitarist. At least that's what my agent told me."

"Your agent?"

"I'm a musician, but I think you already knew that."

"Why do you say that?"

"I saw you admiring my guitar in the back seat when you got in earlier."

"So, that doesn't mean you're a musician."

"Oh I think you know."

"You're not making any sense." I let out a giggle as he raised an eyebrow before looking back at the road. I looked back over at him and saw him yawn and rub his eyes.

"Do you need a break?" He laughed and shook his head.

"You are not driving my car."

"Well what's going to happen when you fall asleep and you wreck your car?"

"Well that's not going to happen."

"How do you know that?" I said crossing my arms and raising an eyebrow.

"Because at the next exit I'm getting off the highway and going to a motel."

"What do you mean you're going to a motel? What about me?"

"Well you can sleep in the car if you want."

"Are you saying you expect me to sleep with you in a motel?"

"I don't think we're that close yet." He smirked as I let out a groan.

"I didn't mean for it to come out like that."

"Good, because I didn't mean it like that either." He started laughing when I folded my arms over my chest and slouched back down in the seat.

"When is the next exit?"

"In a couple miles, so do you think you can wait that long to sleep with me?"

"You're never going to let me live that down either are you?"

"No, I don't think I will it's just too funny to let it go." I smiled and playfully smacked him on his arm. My eyes widened as I realized that I had just flirted with him. I was going on this trip to get away from guys but here I was flirting with the first guy I spent any time with. I could feel him staring at me and I knew he was smirking as well.

"There's the exit." I told him pointing it out as he got into that lane.

"We'll be at the motel in a couple minutes." I nodded as he drove through the small town. He pulled onto the main drag and I saw the motel sign up ahead. He pulled into the motel's parking lot and got out heading to the motel check in. As I sat waiting on him to come back, I looked around and noticed that the motel was done in a western theme. As I was looking around at my surroundings, I heard someone knocking on my window. I looked up to see Xander standing outside motioning for me to come with him. I nodded and grabbed my bag from the backseat as he went around to the trunk and grabbed one of his bags.

"Can you grab my guitar too? I don't want to leave it out here." I nodded before grabbing it as well and following him toward the room he had apparently gotten for us.

"Home sweet home for the night at least." I smiled as he opened the door and held it open for me to enter. I turned on the light and giggled as I saw the western theme room.

"Well isn't this just cozy." That was the only thing I was able to say as I looked around the room.

"Cozy, wouldn't be the word I would use." He said as he threw his bags onto the bed closest to the window.

"What if I wanted the one by the window?"

"No, you don't." I raised my eyebrow as I placed my stuff on the other double bed.

"Oh really." He ignored me as he grabbed one of his bags and headed into the bathroom.

"I'm going to use the bathroom first." He told me closing the door behind him. I fell back on the bed staring at the ceiling. I glanced toward the door as I heard the shower start. It wasn't very long after that I heard him start singing. I smiled to myself as I heard his perfect voice ring out once more. I rolled over and grabbed my purse off the floor where I had dropped it. I got out my phone and saw it was around three in the morning. I sighed and dropped it back in my bag abandoning the call I had planned on making. I rolled back over on the bed continuing to stare at the ceiling, which was painted with a western scene.

"Your turn Blondie." I glanced up to see Xander walking out of the bathroom in pajama pants and a towel around his neck, which he was using to dry his hair. I blushed and grabbed my bag from the floor before brushing past him into the bathroom and closing the door behind me before he had a chance to say anything witty. I put my bag on the sink and pressed my back to the door letting a smile grace my face. I felt some blush rise to my cheeks as I thought of his chiseled body standing there with water, dripping down his chest. I shook my head and turned toward the shower turning it on to the perfect temperature for me. I stepped into the shower letting it rinse off all of the dirt, grime, and all the bad emotions I had gathered throughout the day. I wished for the water to wash away all my fears, but it seemed to just make me realize what they really were. I was alone in this world now and I had made that choice. I knew Xander was right outside the door but that didn't seem to be any comfort to me. I didn't know if I could trust him at all. I knew nothing about this guy yet I was going on a road trip with him to Colorado and sleeping in the same room as him. What in the world was I thinking he could be a rapist for all I knew. I felt my eyes widened as I realized I was here alone with a could be rapist. I quickly turned off the shower and grabbed a towel before starting to dry off. I put on the pajamas I had brought with me and grabbed my bag. I swung the door open and walked straight toward the bed trying not to look at the man lounging on the bed beside mine. I shoved my stuff back in my bag and started walking toward the door.

"Where you going Blondie?" I sucked in my breath and let my hand fall from the door handle. I turned around to see him sitting half way up using his elbows as a support. He raised his eyebrow when I didn't answer but instead I stared at him with a look of horror.

"What's got you so spooked?" He got off the bed and started to walk toward me. When I backed myself up against the door, he stopped and a look of realization crossed his face.

"I'm not going to hurt you." His voice sounded so kind and comforting that I wanted to believe him, but for some reason I couldn't.

"I don't know that." I managed to stutter, but as soon as I said it, I saw the look of hurt cross his features.

"Please just trust me."

"I can't." He sighed and grabbed his coat from the chair by the window.

"I'll sleep out in the car. You can have the room." He told me quietly as he walked past me and out the door closing it tightly behind him. I let out a sigh of relief before going over and tossing my stuff back on the floor. I jumped on the bed and turned on the TV starting to flip through the channels. I ended up watching the news channel and found out that there was a thunderstorm heading toward us here in Warrenton, Missouri. I looked outside and saw that it had started to rain quite intensely. I sighed and looked over at the empty bed beside me. I then heard someone scream in the room beside mine, and someone or something hit the wall behind my bed. I jumped up and put on my jacket before running over to the window and glancing over where Xander's car was sitting. I heard another scream and I groaned before opening the door to see that the rain had picked up and it was now starting to thunder loudly. I pulled my hood up and ran over to where Xander's car was sitting. I tried to open the door but it was locked so I opted for banging on the window. I saw some movement and the door opened. I quickly jumped in and shut the door, locking it behind me. It was then that I realized how cold and wet I was. I looked over to see Xander pull his seat up to an upright position and stare at me expectantly.

"I'm sorry I freaked out and accused you of being a rapist or whatever," He raised an eyebrow but stayed silent as I continued to rant. "I think you should come back inside with me."

"What happened?" He asked some concern crossing his features but mostly it was just amusement.

"Someone screamed in the room next to ours and then something or someone hit the wall and…" I was interrupted by him laughing loudly.

"So you think that someone was being murdered next door?"

"Well yeah." I replied starting to feel foolish, but I wasn't sure why.

"It was probably just the TV."

"There's nothing on the TV like that."

"Well then it was probably just your imagination."

"Please come back inside." I pleaded with him trying to give him my best puppy-dog face I could.

"Fine, but don't accuse me of trying to molest you or kill you ever again."

"Deal." I smiled brightly grabbing his bag from the backseat before going back out into the thunderstorm. I quickly ran toward the motel room and stopped outside waiting on Xander. He shook his head laughing before opening the door and heading inside. Once inside I tossed his bag on the floor and locked the door.

"You're pathetic I hope you know that."

"No, I'm just being cautious." His eyes twinkled as he started to laugh again. He threw himself onto his bed and stretched out.

"Can we go to sleep now? I'm really tired." I nodded and turned out the light before trying to make it over to my bed without tripping over anything. Once I had made it over to my bed, I threw my jacket onto the floor and snuggled into the covers trying to get some warmth back into my body. No sooner had I closed my eyes the same ear-piercing scream rang out in the night. I jumped up in my bed and stared wide-eyed into the darkness. I looked over at Xander who was still asleep in his bed. I glanced around fervently before jumping over on Xander's bed. I heard something hit the wall so I frantically started to push Xander trying to wake him up.

"What?" He answered sleepily trying to wake himself up by rubbing his eyes.

"Did you hear that?" I asked turned on the lamp in between the beds.

"Hear what?" He asked back starting to get annoyed that I had woke him up.

"Some woman screamed then I heard something hit the wall again."

"You really are delusional Blondie. Let me go back to sleep." He rolled onto his side facing away from me. I stayed sitting on his bed and crossed my arms across my chest.

"Turn off the light." I groaned and turned the lamp back off, but still didn't move from where I was sitting.

71

"Why are you still sitting on my bed?" He groaned turning to face me.

"I'm scared." He sighed as he saw my face.

"Of what Blondie? Something that is probably just your imagination?"

"It's not my imagination."

"Well what do you want me to do then?"

"Could you go check to see what's going on?"

"So you want me to go next door and check to see if someone is getting murdered?" I nodded with pleading eyes. He sighed and got out of the bed and headed toward the door.

"Where are you going?" I asked in a panicky voice.

"You just told me to go check next door." He told me in a frustrated voice.

"But that would mean that I would be left in here by myself."

"Blondie you are so confusing." He walked back over to the bed and sat down beside me. He pulled the covers up over his legs and lifted on my side inviting me to get under them.

"I promise I won't molest you or whatever." I smiled and quickly got under the covers with him.

"Thanks Xander." I heard him mutter something under his breath before I closed my eyes again trying to get some sleep before morning came. I woke up to the sound of sirens and the flashing lights that went along with them. I looked beside me and the bed was empty, so I leaned over and grabbed my cell phone out of my bag. It was nine in the morning, so I had only gotten about five hours of sleep. I stretched my arms above my head and wiped the sleep out of my eyes. I clumsily got out of my bed and headed over to the window to see what was going on outside. I pulled back the curtain to see several police cars, an ambulance, a news van, and tons of people walking around.

"What happened?" I asked quietly to no one in particular.

"You were right about the screams." I heard a voice come from behind me. I turned around to see Xander standing in the bathroom doorway.

"What do you mean?" I asked as he came over pulling me away from the window.

"They'll start asking us questions if they see you in the window. Some girl got raped and killed last night in the room next to ours." He told me quietly as he led me over to the bed.

"Oh my goodness. See I told you something was going on."

"Yeah and you wanted to send me over there to get killed, thanks."

"Shouldn't we tell them what we heard?"

"No, then we'll get wrapped up in a big murder trail, and we don't have time for that now, do we?"

"Well I guess not."

"Come on pack your bags and let's go." He threw his bag on the bed beside me along with mine.

"But won't they see us when we go outside to get in the car?"

"We're going out through the back."

"They'll still see us when we go to the car." I told him smugly crossing my arms across my chest staring him down.

"Fine, but just pretend like nothing happened."

"I'm not going to lie to the police."

"Why are you so stubborn?" He asked as he started to throw my stuff in my bag.

"Why are you avoiding the police?"

Chapter Ten

I don't have time to get involved with the police right now. I need to get to Colorado and so do you, and do you really want your parents to see you on the news giving an interview?" He finished throwing all my stuff in my bag zipping it up and tossing it at me. I just nodded and followed him toward the door. He pulled back the curtain some and looked out.

"Looks like we're in luck. Come on Blondie." He grabbed my free hand and pulled me out through the door. I glanced around and saw no one in sight. I furrowed my brow and looked over at Xander who kept pulling me toward the car. He opened up the trunk cringing as it squeaked loudly. He tossed our bags in the back and slowly shut the trunk trying not to make any sound while doing so.

"You do know that by avoiding the police it makes us seem a bit suspicious." I whispered harshly to him as we slowly got into the car trying not to make any sounds.

"Will you just shut up?" He whispered back just as harshly. I heard him mutter a curse as he looked up. I followed his gaze to see two police officers walk out of the room next to ours and the reporters following close behind them. Xander turned the car on and started to pull out of the parking space, but the police officer put his hands up motioning for us to stop. Xander put on the brakes and rolled down his window.

"Did you hear anything last night?" I opened my mouth to answer him but was interrupted by Xander.

"No, my wife and I were preoccupied if you know what I mean." Xander put his hand over on my leg and squeezed it lightly smiling at the officer.

"Well thank you for your time." He nodded at us and waved for us to go on. Xander taking his foot off the brake turned in his seat to back out of the parking lot onto the road.

"What was that all about?" I removed his hand off my leg glaring at him.

"I told you I didn't want to get involved with the police."

"You never told me why."

"I already told you that I need to get to Colorado and I don't have time for it."

"Why do you need to get to Colorado so fast?"

"I think it's time for the rules I told you to be initiated."

"What in the world are you talking about?"

"Well remember when I told you what you had to do for me to take you to Colorado?"

"Yeah."

"Well I think the no excessive talking rule needs to commence now."

"You're just trying to get me to stop asking you questions about yourself."

"Nothing gets past you Blondie." He smiled as he pulled into the traffic on the highway.

"Then what am I supposed to do?"

"You could take a nap since you didn't get much sleep last night."

"Can I talk again when I wake up?"

"Sure." I shook my head and put the seat back looking around to find a blanket to cover up with. I found one on the floor so I covered myself up drifting off to sleep.

When I woke up there was a lot more traffic on the road and I glanced around at the scenery but saw it still hadn't changed much. I groaned and turned over to face Xander. He wasn't paying any attention to the fact that I had woke up so I glanced at the clock and saw it was around noon.

"I'm hungry." I stated watching to see if I could scare Xander. He just laughed and shook his head.

"Nice try Blondie. We're getting off at the next exit." He grinned as he saw the scowl on my face. I nodded and put the seat back up to the upright position and tossed the blanket on the back seat.

"Where are we now?" He smiled and shrugged.

"Not sure, but I see your back to talking incisively."

"I've only told you I'm hungry and asked where we were."

"I think I liked it better when you were sleeping."

"Well too bad I'm awake now."

"Where do you want to eat?" He asked me as we turned onto the exit.

"You're actually asking me what I want?"

"I won't do it again if you keep that up."

"Fine. I want a salad and some fries."

"Ok then." He shook his head as he pulled into a fast food restaurant. He pulled through the drive thru and waited for the lady to come over the speaker and ask us what we wanted.

"Welcome to Bubba's how may I help you?"

"I want two hamburgers, a large fry, and a large chocolate milkshake. Do you want to change your order?" He asked me the last part.

"I want a chicken sandwich, a medium fry, a small salad, and a medium chocolate milkshake." I had leaned over him so I could get close enough to the speaker so she could hear me.

"Is that all for you?"

"Yes." He answered putting his arm around my waist keeping me where I was.

"That will be $10.50 please pull around to the next window."

"Do you have any money Blondie?" He pulled around to the next window his arm still firmly placed around my waist.

"In the trunk." I smirked at him trying to pull free from his grasp.

"Since you're right there can you reach in my back pocket and get my wallet out?"

"Can I what?" I raised my eyebrow in amusement.

"Will you just get it?" I sighed as he lifted up some so I could reach his back pocket. I finally reached under him and pulled it out handing it to him.

"Will you let go of me now?" He smirked and let me sit back down in my own seat as he handed the money to the lady at the window. She in exchange handed us our food.

"Eat up Blondie." He told me as he handed me my food and pulled away from the restaurant. He pulled my drink out, put it in one of the cup holders, and got out my salad starting to eat it as Xander made his way back to the highway.

"Do you want your hamburger?" I handed it to him as soon as he nodded.

"Is that good?" I nodded and continued to eat my food.

"What about yours?" He nodded and held it out offering for me to take a bite. I obliged and took a small bite nodding my head in agreement with him. I finished off my salad and then started on my chicken sandwich. I could feel him staring at me and I knew exactly what he wanted, so I offered him a bite so we would then be even. I then had to wrestle it away from him as he decided that mine was better than his and he wanted all of it. I couldn't help but smile and laugh at him and the playful side he brought out in the both of us.

"Do you know where we are?" I asked finishing off my milkshake trying to glance around to recognize scenery.

"Get out the map in the glove compartment." I obliged opening it up so we could both see it.

"This is where we stopped at the motel." He told me pointing out Warrenton, Missouri.

"Is this where we stopped to eat?" I pointed out Boonville, Missouri.

"So we should be somewhere near Marshall Junction then."

"Do you think by tonight we should be in Kansas?" He nodded and motioned for me to put the map back away.

"Do you want to stop for the night when we stop for dinner here in about six hours?"

"That sounds good, but aren't you in a hurry to get to Colorado?" I asked instantly regretting that I brought it up again.

"You're just not going to let that go are you?"

"No, I want to know why."

"I just want to get there as soon as possible."

"Why?" He slammed his hands against the steering wheel and quickly pulled the car over to the side of the road.

"Will you just let it go?!" He unbuckled his seat belt, got out of the car, and walked around to the trunk.

"Let what go? You won't tell me anything!" I yelled after him.

"You don't need to know everything about me, so mind your own business!" He yelled from where he was standing at the back of the car. I turned around to see him slam his hands down on the trunk of the car causing the whole car to rock. I jumped in my seat as he hit the back of the trunk again. I turned around in time to see him kick one of the tires. I got out of the car and walked slowly over to where he was now standing his hands resting on the trunk and his head hung.

"What are you doing?" I almost laughed at myself at how childish I sounded at that moment, but I couldn't help it he was starting to scare me.

"I needed some fresh air." I saw him grit his teeth trying to stay calm.

"You could've just put the window down." I cringed at my stupidity as the words came tumbling out of my mouth.

"Why don't you just keep your stupid opinions to yourself?!" He cried out slamming his hands down on the trunk.

"I'm sorry." I told him quietly coming to his side and hesitantly placing my hand on his back. I felt him tense then relax as I rubbed small circles on his back.

"Ugh, I'm sorry too. You're just curious and I shouldn't get mad at you considering you know nothing about me." I just nodded not wanting to say anything stupid and make everything worse like I seemed to have a habit of doing.

"Can we get back in the car it's starting to rain?" I asked him as I felt rain start to hit my face. He chuckled as he looked over at me trying to pull the hood up on my hoodie over my head.

"You amuse me Blondie." I glared at him grabbing his arm trying to pull him toward the car, but I wasn't able to budge him.

"Come on the rain is really picking up now." I whined still trying to pull him toward the car.

"This is a warm rain so why are you complaining?" He asked me pulling me toward him.

"It's still rain and it's getting me wet and I don't like it."

"Isn't rain supposed to be all romantic for you girls?" I couldn't help but blush as he pulled me closer to him.

"Why's that?"

"Isn't it every girl's dream to be kissed in the rain?" He smirked leaning closer to me.

"Not every girl's."

"So it's not yours then?" I shook my head as he leaned closer his lips almost touching mine.

"No." I managed to stutter right before he placed his lips over mine. My eyes fluttered close and everything disappeared including the rain that was now mixing in with our kiss. I had been kissed before, but never in the rain and never like this. My eyes snapped open and I pulled free from his grasp as I realized what I was doing.

"What's wrong?" He asked as I turned quickly around and started walking down the road.

"Blondie!" He yelled after me as I started to run down the side of the road. I chanced a glance behind me to see him to start running after me.

"Go away!" I yelled over my shoulder as I heard him starting to catch up to me. I felt him grab my waist and I lost my footing sending me backwards into him, who fell backwards onto the ground bringing me down with him.

"What's wrong with you?" He asked me keeping a firm grip on me as the rain fell in a downpour around us.

"Let me go." I struggled to get free from him.

"Was I that bad a kisser? If I was, you can tell me it won't hurt my feelings or anything." I tried to keep myself from smiling but he seemed to be able to make me smile even when I didn't want to.

"Let me get up." I immediately stood up and stepped back as soon as he let go.

"I suppose you're not going to tell me what that little outburst back there was?" He asked me as we headed back toward the car with me a couple steps in front of him, so that when he tried to walk beside me I just sped up. I heard him groan and knew he had given up. When we reached the car, I quickly got in and glared out the window waiting on him to get in so we could leave.

"At least she isn't going to ask me any annoying questions anytime soon." I heard him mumble to himself as he started up the car and pulled back onto the highway. I snorted causing him to glance over at me.

"You're not that lucky."

"So are you planning to still talk to me?"

"No."

"You're talking to me right now." I could tell he was smirking without even looking at him.

"Will you stop smirking it's getting on my nerves?"

"This smirk is my trade mark, so that's a no."

"You really are infuriating you know that?"

"My father tells me that all the time."

"You have a father?!" I asked placing my hand over my heart in fake astonishment.

"Yes, I have a mother too."

"Let me guess you're running away?" He raised an eyebrow at me before looking back at the road.

"Why are you avoiding talking about that kiss we had back there?"

"I am not."

"I think you are actually. I mean you're making up random stuff about me just to take the focus off what happened."

"I'm not making up random stuff. I think that's why you want to get to Colorado so badly, why you're avoiding the police."

"See you're still avoiding it. Why are you avoiding what's inevitable?"

"Why are you?" I countered still trying to get the attention off myself. He opened his mouth and then closed it, but I knew I wasn't going to win that easily. He opened his mouth again this time to say something, but a muffled ringing interrupted him.

"What's that?" My eyes widened as I looked back at the trunk of the car.

"My cell. Pull over." He pulled over and I grabbed the keys from the ignition and ran around to the back praying that it would keep ringing. I quickly opened the trunk and grabbed my purse out before slamming the trunk back closed and getting back in the car. I threw the keys at Xander and started to rummage through my purse for the cell. I pulled it out smiling but the smile quickly faded as I saw who was on the other end.

"Who is it?" I handed him the phone so he could see for himself.

Chapter Eleven

J ason." I told him, as a look of understanding crossed his face.

"Well let's see what your ex has to say." My eyes widened as he answered the phone. I went to grab the phone from him, but he wouldn't let me.

"Claire's phone, this is Xander." He smirked as he turned up the volume so I could hear what Jason was saying.

"Who are you?" I heard a confused Jason say.

"Xander give me my phone back." I lunged at him trying to get it back, but he just grabbed me by my waist again so that I couldn't move.

"No, I don't think I'll answer that. What do you want with Claire?" He smirked as I stopped struggling and settled for glaring at him.

"I'm her boyfriend and I want to know where she is."

"I didn't ask you who you were because I know who you are, but let's discuss that issue. From what I've heard you two are over, so why would you be calling her?"

"Who are you?!" I heard Jason yell and I knew he was getting angry.

"I already told you I'm not answering that."

"Let me talk to Claire." I heard Jason spit out trying to stay calm but not succeeding.

"Claire doesn't want to talk to you." I heard some things clatter in the background, so I knew that Jason had thrown something.

"Xander just let me talk to him." I said quietly as I started to feel bad for Jason.

"Stop feeling bad for him. You're too nice Claire." Xander told me his eyes full of care and concern for me.

"Was that Claire?!" I heard Jason ask. I let my eyes plead with Xander to give me the phone.

"Yes, and we have to go." Xander closed the phone his eyes never leaving mine.

"Why wouldn't you let me talk to him?"

"You don't need to talk to him. You need to move on."

"Move on?! Where do you want me to move on to? YOU?!" I had wriggled my way out of my grasp and was now staring at him with disbelief.

"You are the one running away because of him, so why don't you do what you've set out to do?!"

"Don't even think you know what I'm feeling?"

"I don't have to know what you're feeling because I know what I'm feeling!"

"What do you mean by that?!" I yelled back grabbing my phone from his hand.

"Forget I even said it." He said turning the key in the ignition.

"No, we're going to talk about it." I said stubbornly turning the key off.

"No, we are not." He turned the key back on glaring at me.

"Oh, I think we are." I said turning the key back off again.

"You don't need to know!" He yelled turning the key back on.

"I want to know!" I pleaded trying to turn the key back off but couldn't as he placed his hand on mine making sure it wouldn't move.

"I don't want you to know for a reason, so please respect my wishes' Claire."

"You said my name." He nodded letting my hand fall to my side before putting the car in drive and pulling back onto the highway. I moved back to my seat slowly and buckled back up rubbing the hand he had a hold of unconsciously trying to get that instant feeling of warmth he had given me by that one touch to go away.

"Why didn't you just let me talk to him?" I sighed finally getting up enough nerve to face him. He chose to ignore me and kept driving down the highway.

"Take a nap." He told me simply not even bothering to look at me.

"Why should I?" I countered.

"I decided we aren't going to sleep in a motel tonight, so I need you to get your rest so you can drive tonight."

"What? You're actually going to let me drive your precious car?"

"Yes, now go to sleep."

"I guess it's not that precious since you decided to beat up on it earlier."

"Will you just go to sleep?" He snapped speeding up and passing the line of cars in front of us. I glared at him, grabbed the blanket out of the back, and snuggled up as I had done this morning. I figured I could get about five hours of sleep since it was five o'clock.

"I'll see you in five hours." I told him quietly as I drifted off to sleep dreaming of what was to come.

I was only asleep for three hours when Xander woke me up. I rolled over pulling the blanket over my head trying to get away from him. I swatted his hand away from me as he shook my shoulder trying to wake me up. I groaned as he pulled the blanket off me and threw it on the backseat.

"Your phone is ringing, wake up." I groaned and blindly searched for my purse. I found it and grabbed my cell out of it opening it up and answering it.

"Hello?" I answered groggily rubbing the sleep out of my eyes trying to wake myself up. Xander chuckled as he rolled down the window my eyes shooting open as the cold night air hit my face.

"Claire, its Allison. Where are you?"

"We're almost in Kansas." Xander told me as I glanced over at him.

"Kansas, why?"

"Jason and Brad are looking for you."

"What?! Together?!"

"Yeah I know we were as shocked as you are."

"Do they know where I'm at?"

"Well they know you're going to Colorado to find Sophie, so that's where they're heading."

"I don't want them to find me though." I whined laying my head back on the seat.

"We're following them, so just keep us updated on where you're at and we'll keep them as far away from you as possible."

"Who's we?"

"Elizabeth, Ben, and me."

"There's no way they are going to be able to catch up to us."

"I wouldn't be so sure about that."

"What do you mean by that?"

"They took Brad's Corvette and they aren't really obeying any speed limits."

"Well how are you guys keeping up then?"

"We're not we just have a tracker on them."

"How did you get a tracker on them?"

"We're not rich for nothing."

"Don't remind me."

"Jason said something about you being kidnapped by a guy?"

"I wasn't kidnapped."

"So you are with a guy then?"

"Yes." I glanced over at Xander.

"Is he cute?"

"I have to go Allison, so call me if you need anything."

"He totally is, isn't he?"

"Bye Allison." I hung up the phone despite her protests and I tossed it back in my purse.

"What was that all about?"

"Well Jason thought I was kidnapped no thanks to you. So he and Brad teamed up to come find me."

"So, your exes are coming after you, what's the big deal?"

"I don't want them to find me." I told him quietly.

"Well what do you want me to do about it?"

"I don't know."

"Give me your cell." My head snapped up to look at him as he held out his hand for my cell.

"Why?"

"Just give it to me." I cautiously handed it over to him as he dialed a number.

"What are you doing?" He held up his hand signaling for me to shut up.

"It's Xander. I have two males in a Corvette following me."

"I'll need their names and a description of the car." I heard a feminine voice say on the other end.

"Jason Perry and Brad Widford. The Corvette is blue with white racing strips going up the front. The license plate reads 2HOT4U." I told Xander letting him relay the information to the woman on the other end of the phone.

"Thanks Gloria." He hung up the phone and handed it back to me.

"What was that all about and who's Gloria?"

"She's my ex-girlfriend and she's going to help get rid of them."

"What do you mean by get rid of them?!" My octaves rising above their normal pitch as I said this.

"They're not going to hurt them, just keep them busy for a while."

"So, are you and Gloria close then?"

"She just owes me a favor." He told me not bothering to look at me once again.

"How can she do that though?"

"Let's just say she comes from quite an influential family."

"We're your families' friends?"

"You could say that."

"That means that your family would be just a rich or influential." He looked over at me and sighed before looking back over at the road.

"You just don't give up do you Blondie?"

"No."

"Why don't you want them to find you?"

"I thought you'd be happy that I'm trying to move on." I snapped starting to get annoyed with him avoiding my questions.

"They're still your friends."

"Are we in Kansas?" I asked trying to look around at the darkness.

"Yeah Kansas City is up ahead." I nodded grabbing the blanket from the backseat trying to go back to sleep.

"Goodnight then."

"How about we stop at a motel for the night."

"I thought you didn't want to tonight."

"I changed my mind." I sighed as he pulled off the highway heading into Kansas City to find a motel for the night.

"Where are we going to stay tonight?" I asked looking around at the tall buildings that surrounded me.

"How about a five star hotel?" His eyes sparkled as he looked over at me.

"I guess this is where I pay my share rule comes in right?"

"No, I'll pay."

"You don't have that much money with you."

"Snooping in my wallet were you?" He asked laughing.

"You were the one that made me 'snoop' in it."

"I have some connections let's just put it that way."

"What's up with you and connections?" He just smiled before pulling into the parking garage for one of the hotels lining the road.

"Get your stuff." He told me as he got out of the car proceeding to get his stuff from the trunk. I grabbed my stuff out of the back right before he closed the trunk and walked away toward an elevator leaving me to look around at my surroundings. I looked up to see him waiting in the elevator for me, so I picked up my stuff and ran toward him just making it into the elevator before the doors closed.

"I think I'm going to have to keep you on a leash or you're going to get lost." He commented as the elevator brought us up the side of the building looking out over the city.

"What hotel are we in?" I asked him still looking around.

"Don't worry about it." I heard a ding and the elevator opened revealing a long glass hallway leading across the street to the building beside us.

"I thought that we were already in the hotel?"

"No, just a parking garage." I nodded looking down at the cars passing below us.

"This is amazing." I commented looking around trying to let everything sink in.

"I thought you were rich." He commented back raising an eyebrow.

"I am. I just haven't been here before." He chuckled and grabbed my hand leading me through the rest of the tunnel toward the door on the other end. When we reached the other side, he opened the door to reveal a huge atrium below us as we stood on a balcony over looking it.

"Come on." He proceeded to lead me toward another elevator.

"Don't we have to check in?" I asked looking down at the check in desk in the atrium below.

"No."

"Why not?" I asked curiously, as we got in the elevator. He pushed the button for the 20th floor and the elevator doors closed taking us up to that floor.

"I already told you." The elevator doors opened up revealing a long hallway with two doors on either end of the hallway.

"Is this where we're staying?" He laughed before leading me toward the door on the right. He let go of my hand that I hadn't even realized he still had a hold of. As soon as he let go I felt the same warmth I had felt earlier. He reached in his back pocket taking out his wallet and took out a card, which he put in the door, which unlocked with a ding.

"Welcome home." He told me pushing the door open to reveal a huge room lavishly decorated.

"Not bad." I told him tossing my bags on the floor, running over to the couch, and flinging myself onto it.

"Enjoying yourself?" I nodded glancing around for a remote for the flat screen TV that graced the wall in front of the couch.

"This is a definite improvement from your car and the last motel we stayed at."

"Plus there won't be any murders in the room next to us." My head snapped up to glare at him.

"How did you get that key?"

"I already told you." He answered simply taking his bags with him into one of the rooms, which I assumed was a bedroom.

"Do I get my own bedroom tonight?"

"Yes." He called from inside the room. I jumped off the sofa and grabbed my bags heading toward the door across the hall from his. I opened it to find a king-sized bed in the middle of a huge bedroom. I squealed throwing my bags onto the chair beside the door before jumping onto the bed.

Chapter Twelve

What are you doing?" He asked not bothering to hide the amusement in his voice as he stood in the doorway watching me jump up and down on the bed.

"Sorry, I just always wanted to do that." I smiled sheepishly.

"Once again I thought you were rich."

"Just because I am doesn't mean I can't enjoy myself."

"Right." He walked away down the hall me chasing after him.

"Why aren't you more excited?" I asked a smirk gracing my face as I was still trying to figure him out.

"I've been here before." He told me simply walking into another room. I followed him in to see that we were standing in the bathroom.

"Neat." I said looking around at the vast and once again lavish bathroom.

"I don't know what you're doing, but I'm planning on taking a shower."

"Oh." Blush crept up onto my cheeks as I backed out of the bathroom closing the door on a very amused Xander. I couldn't help but giggle as I skipped back down the hall to the living room. I glanced around and saw there were curtains covering the one wall. I walked over and opened them up to find the whole wall covered with a window that overlooked the city. I heard the water start running and knew that Xander had started his shower. I glanced at the clock and saw it was about eight o'clock and I still hadn't had any supper. I walked over to the kitchen and looked in the fridge to see if there was anything, I could possibly cook for us to eat. I opened it up to see a couple cans of soda and that was it. I sighed and looked around for a phone so I could call room service. I hadn't looked very far when I heard the shower shut off, so I decided I would wait for Xander to see what he wanted to do. I went to my room and grabbed my bag remembering that I hadn't written anything for a while. I got out the book Sophie had given me and laid down on the bed starting to write about everything that had happened so far on this long journey I was taking called life. I couldn't help but giggle to myself as I thought of some of the things that had happened so far. I quickly finished writing down my thoughts as I heard the door to the bathroom open. I threw the book back in my bag and ran out into the hallway to see Xander emerge in just a towel once again.

"What is it with you and towels?" I asked leaning against the doorframe.

"What is up with you staring at me when I'm only wearing a towel?"

"I stare at you other times too." I tried to defend myself but failed miserably as I realized what I had just said.

"Don't worry I stare at you too." He said winking as he walked over to his room. The smile still hadn't left my face when he closed the door behind him. I was able to get in a silent jig before his door opened again.

"We're having dinner at the restaurant downstairs so find something nice to wear."

"I didn't bring anything nice with me."

"Look in your closet I'm sure there's something in there that will fit you." He winked before closing the door again. I furrowed my brows before walking into my room and opening up the closet to reveal a variety of outfits all in my size. I picked out a light-blue sundress that had caught my eye and quickly slipped it on. I glanced around for shoes and saw there were matching flip-flops sitting on the floor among a bunch of other shoes that probably had an outfit that matched it somewhere in there. I glanced in the mirror of the vanity and frowned at how unkempt I looked. My mother would be having a conniption if she was to see me look like this.

"Do I have time to take a quick shower?" I asked Xander threw his door.

"Yeah, the reservations aren't till nine." I nodded and made my way toward the bathroom at the end of the hall. Once inside I peeled off the dress and stepped into the shower letting it wash away all the grime that had built up throughout the day. I smiled as I remembered what had happened the last time I had taken a shower, and how I had accused him of being a rapist. I turned off the water, wrapped a large towel around my body, and went over to the sink. I wiped the steam off the mirror and started to brush my hair with a brush I had found on the counter. I glanced around and found a hair dryer, so I started to dry and style my hair. Once I had finished, I slipped the dress and the matching shoes back on and walked out of the bathroom toward my room. Xander was still in his room so I decided I had some time to put on some much needed make-up. Normally I wouldn't have bothered but I felt like I needed to impress Xander. I hated to admit it to myself, but I had the tiniest bit of a crush on him. Finishing my make-up, I heard my phone start to ring again. I glanced at my purse and sighed going over to see who it was. It was Allison.

"What?"

"Oh is that how it is?"

"Allison." I said impatiently.

"Jason and Brad are in a jail in Missouri."

"What?" I asked astonished.

"There was like a huge police chase and everything."

"Are they ok?" I heard Xander knock on my door so I went over and opened it motioning for him to come in.

"You look gorgeous." He told me giving me a once over.

"Thanks." I blushed but put up my hand as he started to say something again.

"Is that the guy?"

"Yes, are they ok?" She still hadn't answered my question.

"Yeah, but all of our parents are now involved."

"What?!" I almost screamed.

"Yeah, so now they have a search party out for you since Jason and Brad told the police you were kidnapped."

"This is not happening." I groaned falling back onto the bed beside where Xander was sitting.

"You might want to turn on the TV though."

"Where's the remote?" I asked Xander running into the living room with him close behind me. He grabbed a remote from the kitchen counter and tossed it to me.

"What channel?" I asked Allison.

"Any news channel." I turned on the TV and saw a news report that made my heart skip a beat.

"Early this morning a young girl was raped and murdered in this motel in Warrenton, Missouri. We have two suspects and possible runaways that fled the scene." I gasped as the TV showed me and Xander pulling away from the motel. "If anyone sees these two people whom we have identified as runaway Claire Walker and Xander..." The TV shut off and I looked over at Xander to see him holding the remote in his hand looking incredibly angry.

"We need to leave now." He grabbed my free arm trying to drag me toward the door.

"What's going on?" Allison asked.

"I don't know." I told her back honestly.

"I need to get my purse it has my book." I told Xander desperately.

"Your book?" He stopped and turned to stare at me.

"I'm writing a book and I have to get it." I told him nervously.

"Go get it and hurry." I ran toward the room, grabbed my purse, and ran back out just in time to hear a loud pounding on the door.

"Crap." Xander muttered grabbing me by the arm and pulling me down the hall as the voices on the other side of the door got louder and the knocks more frequent.

"What's going on?" I asked Xander starting to panic as he pulled me into his room shutting and locking the door.

"What do you think?" He snapped looking around for something frantically.

"Allison I think I have to go." I told her hanging up the phone and putting it in my purse.

"Where is it?" Xander bellowed throwing things around the room still searching.

"Where's what?" I winced as a chair hit the wall.

"The key." He took a deep breath and turned to look at me.

"What key?" His eye widened, as he pushed past me seeming to remember where 'the key' was. I turned around to see him dump the contents of the vase, sitting on the table by the door, out. The last thing to fall out was a small key, which he quickly picked up and ran toward the other side of the room grabbing my arm and pulling me with him.

"Push the bed out of the way." I quickly followed his lead pushing the bed to the side to reveal a vent, which he unlocked with the key. He grabbed something off the bedside table and put it in his pocket before pushing me down the vent and following me, closing and locking the vent behind us.

"What do you want me to do now?" I asked trying to look around in the small space we were sitting in.

"Go that way." He pointed to my left and pushed me that way. I started crawling through the vent carefully.

"Which way now?" I asked as we came upon an intersection in the vent system.

"Is there an opening?"

"What?" I asked looking back at him as he rolled his eyes motioning for me to go forward some. I looked where I was once sitting and saw a vent, which he moved out of the way.

"It leads to the garage come on." He looked around before lowering himself down onto the ground below. I sighed before lowering myself down through the vent. I felt Xander place his hands around my waist and lower me the rest of the way to the ground.

"Thanks, where are we?" I asked looking around seeing that we weren't in the garage.

"The garage is across the road we are in the maid quarters."

"I thought you said it led to the garage." I whispered harshly as he pulled me over to the window.

"It does." He opened up the window and pointed to the garage across the road. I looked down and saw the tunnel we had taken from the garage.

"Do you expect me to walk across that?"

"Yes." He smiled widely before putting his leg over the edge of the window and stepping out onto the ledge below. He scooted over and stuck his hand out for me to grab. I grabbed his hand stepping out the window onto the ledge closing my eyes tightly.

"I'm gonna die." I kept repeating over and over to myself keeping my eyes firmly shut as Xander led me slowly along the ledge.

"You're not going to die because we're here." I could hear the amusement in his voice as I opened one eye making sure he wasn't lying to me. In front of us was the tunnel so he stepped down carefully onto the ceiling of it. He put his arms up and I grasped his hands as he carefully brought me down to where he was standing.

"So how are we going to get in there now?" I asked keeping a firm hold on Xander as I looked around seeing just how far up we were. He bent down slowly bringing me with him and removed a vent cover.

"I'll go first." I let go of him as he jumped down into the hallway below. I glanced around quickly and closed my eyes before jumping down into his arms. I opened my eyes to see his face a few inches away from mine, but he wasn't looking at me but everywhere else.

"What are you doing?" I whispered staring intently at his handsome face.

"Come on." He removed his hands from my waist once again grabbing my hand and running down the hallway toward the other end. As we reached the other end, I heard loud voices coming from the other side of the elevator door. It opened to reveal a family of five smiling at us before heading down the hallway. I smiled back before getting in the elevator with Xander. As the doors closed, I let out the huge breath I had been holding. The elevator seemed to take forever as it made its way slowly down to the level Xander's car was on. The doors finally opened and we stepped out into the garage. I started to walk toward where Xander's car was but he pulled me back quickly.

"What?" I asked in a low whisper. He pointed toward the police car and all the people surrounding his car. I glanced up at him waiting for him to tell me what we were going to do now. He looked around and paused as he evidently saw what he was looking for. He kept his tight grasp on my hand t as he led us slowly toward the exit on the other end away from the police.

"Run." He told me as we got a few feet away from the exit. I looked at him keeping my grip on his hand as I raced toward the door sighing as we made it out of the garage onto the streets of Kansas.

"Where do we go now?" I asked him as he kept walking down the sidewalk away from the building.

"There's a truck stop not far from here."

"And you plan on what?"

"We're hitching a ride the rest of the way to Colorado."

"With a trucker who we don't even know?"

"Yes." He rolled his eyes pulling me with him as he started to walk faster down the sidewalk.

"How far?"

"I saw it right as we got off the highway." I shivered slightly as the night air whipped around me. He noticed and took off his jacket handing it to me to wear. I smiled and thanked him as I put it on snuggling into the warmth of his jacket. He placed his arm around me leading me down the sidewalk.

"What are we going to do?" I sighed snuggling deeper into his jacket and his arms.

"Don't worry about it ok." He rubbed my arm slowly as we kept walking.

"Are we going to be in a lot of trouble?" I asked him quietly looking at my feet. He placed his hand under my chin lifting my head up to look at him.

"No, I'll get us out of this, I promise."

"Why are you being so nice to me?"

"Why would you even ask that?" He looked at me in disbelief pausing before walking again.

"Just answer it."

"You remind me of myself." He had said it so quietly that I couldn't almost hear it, but we both knew I had. I just nodded and continued walking neither of us saying another word to each other.

Chapter Thirteen

It took an hour to reach the truck stop on foot. That hour was very quiet and possibly the longest hour I had ever experienced. When we reached the truck stop, I jumped for joy on the inside considering I was too tired to actually jump. I glanced over at Xander who was walking slowly beside me a determined look on his face. Looking around the truck stop, I saw ten semis sitting around some with lights on some without.

"Which one are we going to hitch a ride with?" I asked Xander as he led me toward the diner on the other side of the parking lot. He opened the door for me and followed me into the diner the bell ringing as we entered. Every head turned to look at us as we entered.

"Maybe this wasn't such a good idea." I whispered to Xander as he placed his hand on the small of my back leading me toward the counter.

"Trust me." He smiled at me pulling as he sat me down on one of the bar stools before walking away.

"Where are you going?" My eyes widened as I watched him walk away from me telling me to stay where I was. I watched him go over and sit down with a man in the corner of the restaurant. As Xander talked to the man, I felt very aware that everyone was staring at me and that I was the only woman in the entire place. I kept my gaze on Xander as he continued talking. At one point Xander pointed over at me and they both smiled and waved at me as I managed to give a small smile. Xander shook the man's hand and walked back over to me.

"We need to go." He told me quietly placing his hands around my waist lifting me off the stool and guiding me away out the door we had came in moments before.

"Well?" I followed him trying to keep up with his fast pace.

"He knows who we are, and is willing to take us to Denver."

"Is he going to turn us in?"

"No, one look at you and he knew that you weren't any part of it."

"What about you?"

"Here we are." We were standing by a huge blue semi truck. He opened the door and helped me up in the truck before getting in himself and closing the door behind him. He sat down on the passenger seat and brought me onto his lap his arms circling my waist. I sighed deciding there was no reason to struggle so I laid my head against his chest listening to his steady heartbeat. My eyes started to drift close but they snapped open when the door opened and the man Xander was talking to inside stepped into the truck.

"I'm Jon." He stuck his hand out for me to shake which I did hesitantly.

"I'm Claire." I replied as he nodded still smiling. He must have been in his late twenties, which surprised me some. His blonde hair was tied in the back only reaching to the collar of his flannel shirt.

"You two look like you've been through a lot so why don't you get a goodnight sleep in the back." He grinned toothily nodding toward the back where there was a bed. I smiled gratefully and slipped into the back while Xander stayed up front talking some with the man. I turned on the light above my head and got out my book to write some since I wasn't quite ready to go to sleep. I lay back on the bed carefully not comfortable with my surroundings yet. I poised my pencil and began to write about my every thought and feeling I've had in the past twenty-four hours.

After finishing, I closed the book looking up to see Xander looking back at me from the front seat. He patted Jon on the back before walking toward me and sitting down on the bed beside me. He placed his hand on my leg rubbing small circles with his thumb.

"How are you doing back here?"

"I'm fine; I'm starting to get a little tired though."

"Well go to sleep then." He smiled at me pushing some hair out of my face.

"Thank you for your jacket by the way." I went to take it off to give it to him.

"Keep it; it looks better on you anyway." I smiled and snuggled back into it taking in the scent that still lingered. I placed my book back in my purse and I noticed him watching my every move. Scooting over some Xander slid under the covers beside me slipping off his shoes in the process. I laid my head on his chest my hand lying beside it rising with his every breath.

"What's your favorite color?" I listened to his chuckle rumble throughout his chest and through me.

"Green. Let me guess yours is pink?"

"Yeah. Are you close with your family?"

"Just with my sister."

"Is she who you're going to go see in Colorado?"

"Yes, I figured I'd stay with her for a while."

"Any particular reasons why?" He sighed and shook his head.

"What was your childhood like?" I didn't bother commenting on him changing the subject again.

"I was daddy's little princess and my mother tried her hardest to bring me up as the perfect young lady who would be the perfect trophy wife. When I was nine, my mom had a miscarriage losing my little brother, who was going to follow in my father's footsteps and become a doctor to take over the family business. My father then decided that it would then be my job to take over for him, so all through middle school and high school I was to do nothing but train to go to college and be a doctor just like him. My mother of course had to keep me up with being put out into society as well. Basically it was all very hectic and it sucked." I sighed looking up at him who was staring intently at me. He leaned down his lips meeting mine in a soft kiss. I pulled back after a minute my eyes still closed trying to remember every second. My eyes fluttered open full of questions.

"Are your boyfriends' jealous people?" I giggled and nodded as he groaned. "Don't worry about them."

"That's real comforting." I placed my hand on his arm and squeezed lightly in what was supposed to be a comforting gesture.

"Checking out my muscles?" He flexed, smirking as I started to giggle.

"What muscles?" I let out a loud laugh as he pinned me to the bed starting to tickle me. Jon glanced back and shook his head laughing before turning back to the road.

"Say it." He ordered me still tickling me un-mercilessly.

"You have the biggest muscles ever!" I giggled uncontrollably as he stopped tickling me, smiling widely down at me.

"Don't ever forget that." I rolled my eyes and nodded trying to stop giggling and keep a straight face, which I was failing miserably at. I pushed him off me so that he rolled over onto his side of the bed.

"How was your childhood?" I asked him as soon as I had calmed down.

"About the same as yours." I rolled my eyes at his lack of details.

"So you had to come out in society too?" I actually succeeded in keeping a straight face as I asked this. He rolled his eyes before looking up at Jon.

"We'll be in Denver in about six hours." Jon told us as he continued to drive down the highway. I glanced at the clock and saw we had been on the road for two hours already.

"How about we get some sleep." I nodded and snuggled into his arms letting my eyes flutter close and drift off to sleep.

I woke up to the sound of Xander's soft breathing next to my ear. I slowly opened my eyes and turned my head slightly to see him sound asleep his arms still wrapped tightly around my waist. I looked up toward the front to see sunlight pouring into the cab. I carefully moved Xander's arms off from around me and sat up on the bed. I tiptoed toward where Jon was sitting and tapped him lightly on the shoulder.

"How many more hours till we get to Denver?" I whispered trying not to wake Xander up who had rolled over to face the wall.

"We should be there in the hour." I nodded thanking him before going back to sit down on the bed. I grabbed my purse from the floor and got out my book once more along with a pencil. I looked over at Xander smiling as I started to write more. I felt Xander's arms wrap around my waist and him kiss my neck softly.

"Is this the book?" I nodded as he looked over my shoulder.

"We'll be in Denver in a half hour." He nodded trying to read over my shoulder.

"Are you sure writing is something you want to get into?" I glanced at him before nodding.

"It's the one thing that makes me happy and makes me feel like I'm actually doing something important in this world." He seemed to take my answer to heart as he nodded slowly seeming to understand.

"I get that, but what makes you think that you will actually be able to become a writer?" I pulled back from him turning around to face him.

"I don't know I just thought I'd take a chance."

"You need to have more confidence or you'll never make it."

"What makes you the expert on becoming a writer?" He seemed to avoid my gaze before getting up and sitting down next to Jon in the front. I sighed and looked down at my book, which just needed the final touches for it to be done completely. I really didn't know what made me think I could become a writer when there were so many aspiring writers in this world trying to get the same exact spot. Luckily, for all of us there can never be enough writers because everyone has a different perspective and a different way of writing that might appeal to someone else more than another's. I sighed as I put my finishing touches on what I believed to be my own happy ending. I glanced up at Xander, which only made me sigh more as I wrote the last sentence and closed my book knowing that my happy ending probably would never come.

"Where would you like me to drop you two off at?"

"Civic Center Park." Xander answered before I could even think of anywhere.

"Well we're about to hit some traffic so it might take a while to get there." As I watched Xander talk, my heart skipped a beat. Looking down I saw some of my stuff had fallen out of my purse so I picked them up placing them back in my purse. I got out my phone and saw that my battery was almost dead so I turned it off so I could call Sophie later.

"Looks like we're in luck, the traffic is clearing out." Jon glanced back at me with a toothy grin. I smiled back pulling Xander's jacket around me tighter out of instinct. It wasn't that Jon was a creepy guy it was just that I was coming very aware of my surroundings now that Xander wasn't as close to me.

"Here we are."

"Thanks Jon." I walked to the front next to Xander thanking him for the ride and getting out of the semi with the help of Xander. Xander closed the door and hit it a couple times signaling that he could leave. As he left we both waved goodbye before turning toward each other.

"You probably should call Sophie now so she can come pick you up." My head snapped up to look at Xander who was avoiding my stare.

"You mean you're not coming with me?"

"No." He finally looked me in the eye his features softening.

"So this is it then?" He nodded brushing a tear of my cheek that had managed to fall without my knowledge.

"I hope you understand." I shook my head looking down at my feet as if they were the most interesting things in the world.

"Here's your jacket." I went to take it off but he stopped me.

"It's yours." He told me softly, placing his thumb under my chin lifting it up so that our faces we were only a few centimeters away from each other.

"Please don't leave me." I pleaded with him as more tears managed to fall. He kissed the tears away before kissing my lips just as softly.

"Goodbye Claire." He kissed me once more before rushing away. I slowly opened my eyes hoping he was still there but to my dismay, he wasn't. I hastily wiped away my tears before walking over to a bench and sitting down. Opening up my purse, I grabbed my phone and turned it back on. Pushing the number one on my speed dial, I heard the phone start to ring.

"Sophie, can you come get me?" I said as soon as I heard her pick up.

"Claire, where are you?"

"I'm at the Civic Center Park in Denver."

"I thought I told you not to come after me."

"Please just come get me." I pleaded as the tears began to fall uncontrollably.

"I'll be there in an hour, so stay put."

"Ok." I closed the phone and let the handholding it fall to my side. My shoulders began to shake as sobs racked my body. I don't know whom I was fooling thinking that I could possibly have a happy ending especially with someone like him. I knew nothing about him, but somehow I had become quite attached to him, and I had fallen completely in love with him. I had just let him walk out of my life without even trying to stop him. I felt a hand on my shoulder causing me to jump, looking up to see Sophie's kind face. I latched onto her never wanting to let go.

"What happened?" She asked in a soothing voice as she rubbed my back.

"I ran away." My voice came out muffled as my face was buried in her shoulder.

"That much was obvious Claire." I pulled back some to look her in the eye.

"Can we go home?"

"Your home or mine?"

"You are my home." I told her quietly before standing up to follow her toward her car.

"Do you want to talk about it?" Sophie finally asked as she drove through the streets of Denver.

"There's nothing to talk about." I kept my gaze away from hers, as I was afraid of what might happen if I broke down again.

"I saw the news Claire." I sighed risking a glance at her.

"Has anyone called you?"

"Allison called me."

"Well you should know everything then."

"I want to hear it from you though."

"I don't feel like talking about it Sophie."

"Maybe later then." I knew she wasn't going to give up that easily.

"Why don't you tell me about what happened to you?" I finally managed to ask.

"I ran away." I glared at her causing her to laugh.

"Sophie." I warned letting her know my patience was very thin at this point.

"I hitchhiked the entire way till I met a nice guy who was heading in the same direction I was and he took me the rest of the way."

"Are you mocking me?" I asked her harshly.

"No Claire, I'm not."

"Fine." I motioned for her to continue.

"He was heading to Colorado to take some business' courses. He wanted to open his own store, so I told him about how I always wanted to open a bookstore. He loved the idea and decided to open a bookstore with me. I hoped you would be able to figure it out when you heard the name." I nodded smiling as I remembered when I had finally figured out what it meant, and I knew that she was safe.

"Even though I told you I didn't want you to come I kind of hoped you would." She finally admitted as she pulled onto a dirt road that I suppose led to her house.

"Is this where you live?" She smiled and nodded as we pulled up to a cabin overlooking a pond and the mountains in the distance.

"Derek's parents let us use it since it's just their vacation home."

"They're fine with you two living here?" I asked in shock getting out of the car and looking around at the beautiful scenery.

"I didn't want to tell you like this, but Derek and I are married." I whipped around to look at her in shock.

"Why didn't you tell me?"

"Well I was going to, but I didn't know how." I sighed before walking over and hugging her tightly.

"I'm so happy for you, and I can't wait to meet him."

"He'll be home in a couple hours. He just has to close up the store." I nodded as she led me toward her beautiful home. I walked up the stairs onto the deck that wrapped around the cabin.

"This is beautiful." I walked over to the railing that overlooked the mountains in the distance. The sun was starting to set and the colors were like nothing I had ever seen.

"It is, isn't it?" She smiled putting her arm around me letting me lay my head on her shoulder as we watched the sun set behind the mountains.

Chapter Fourteen

CLAIRE!" I ran out the door of Sophie's house toward Allison who was racing toward me. I burst out laughing as she tripped on the first step falling onto me causing me to fall as well. I heard chuckling behind us so I turned to see Derek and Sophie leaning against the railing his arm wrapped loosely around her. Over the past couple of days, I had made myself at home with the newly wed couple. Derek was wonderful man who treated Sophie like a queen, and I couldn't help but admit that Sophie had great taste in men. I always joke around with Derek about letting me meet his older brother because if he was this good looking and wonderful I could only imagine how great his brother was. He always laughed and told me he would most defiantly set the two of us up.

"We brought you your stuff that they found at the hotel." Elizabeth said walking toward us my bags gracing her arms. She threw them to the side as Allison and I held open our arms signaling for her to join us. I looked up at Sophie who laughed and ran into our arms as we all reunited hopefully for the last time. There was a cabin just down the road that I planned on buying so that I could be close to Sophie. Allison and Elizabeth planned to stay with me during the summer and winter breaks. Ben was with Jason and Brad who were currently trying to find an apartment they could rent for a couple months in Denver. I hadn't seen them yet, but there were dinner plans tonight where I would finally be able to see them again. I was anxious to see them after everything that had happened. The charges had been dropped against Xander and me when they had found the real killer. It still freaked me out some that someone was murdered in the room next to mine. My parents knew where I was at, but they didn't seem to care anymore especially since my mother was now pregnant. I felt sorry for the kid and everything that he or she would have to go through to be the next prodigy. Of course, I would be the wonderful sister who would be the much-needed relief from our parents. Sophie had made a deal with her parents and was going to get her GED while running the bookstore with Derek. Overall, the last couple of days had been quite hectic.

"Let's go inside." Derek said grabbing my bags and heading inside the cabin. I got up dusting off my pants before helping the other three up.

"Have you heard from him?" Allison asked me as we were walking inside.

I sighed, falling into the nearest chair by the fireplace. They all sat down on the sofa and chairs surrounding the fireplace.

"No, and I don't think I really care anymore." I knew that they all saw through my facade but I really didn't care anymore.

"What all happened while you were on your journey to discovering yourself?" Allison mocked sarcastically.

"Not much." It was almost creepy how they all rolled their eyes at the same time.

"Come on. Something had to happen." I ignored Elizabeth's comment and looked into the fire at the flickering flames.

"You girls should start getting ready; we're leaving in an hour to meet the boys." Derek came into the room wrapping his arms around Sophie's shoulders before kissing her on the head. We all awed causing Sophie to blush before throwing a pillow at me, as I was closest. Getting up, pulling Allison and Elizabeth with me, as we went to my room to change and get ready. The restaurant was going to be a semiformal one so Allison had picked up some dresses for us since none of us had bothered bringing anything with us.

"Your parents are going to send the rest of your things over in a moving truck next week." I nodded taking the pink sundress that Allison had laid out on the bed for us to choose from.

"Will you two still be here?" I quickly slipped off my clothes and slipping on the sundress.

"Yeah we should be." I nodded before going into the bathroom to finish my hair and make-up. As I was half way through, I paused wondering why I was even bothering considering there wasn't anyone I wanted to impress.

"You ok in there Claire?" I quickly placed the make-up back in the cabinet and walked out of the bathroom.

"Yeah, why wouldn't I be?"

"Well we're going to have supper with both of your ex-boyfriends in less than an hour. If I was you, I wouldn't be."

"Well you're not me now, are you?" I snapped immediately apologizing before sinking into a chair by the door.

"Its fine you're just a bit stressed which is completely acceptable for the situation you're in." I rolled my eyes as I listened to Allison assess my apparent problems.

"Stop trying to be my psychiatrist."

"It's my job." I rolled my eyes and walked out of the room collapsing into the same chair I was in earlier.

"You're ready to go already?" I smiled as Derek walked into the living room sitting down in the rocking chair across from me.

"Yeah."

"Your phone is charged." He tossed my phone to me, which I smiled gratefully for.

"Thanks it's been weird not having this thing." I told him referring to the cell in my hand, which I was now scanning through the missed calls.

"Anybody important?"

"I'm not sure." I told him as I called my voicemail.

"This is Alexia from Hallford Publishers. We read your book and I must say it's brilliant. Please get back with us as soon as possible so we can discuss the details."

"What is it?" Sophie asked walking into the room as I sat shocked my cell still held up to my ear.

"Hallford Publishers called saying they loved my book."

"But you lost your book." She tried to reason with me.

"Yeah, I lost it." I trailed off as I delved into my thoughts.

"Let's go." Allison's voice snapped me out of my thoughts as she entered the room Elizabeth close behind her. I grabbed Xander's jacket, which I had worn every day, and headed out the door close behind everyone else.

"May I take your coat?" I shook my head as the maître d' at the restaurant offered to take my coat.

"What's up with you and that coat?" Elizabeth asked as she handed over her coat to the maître d'.

"It was his." Allison told her as we were escorted to the table where the boys were already waiting. I shyly approached and sunk further behind the group as I saw the three of them sitting there. I knew I had to get this over with, but I wanted to delay it as much as possible.

"Claire?" I slowly raised my head to see Brad and Jason standing while everyone else at the table was sitting waiting on me to sit. I smiled slightly before sitting down in between Sophie and Allison. The waiter came interrupting the awkward silence between our small group. We all ordered our drinks, but something distracted me as the waiter asked me what I wanted. I glanced behind me to see a girl and a guy laughing a couple tables away. There was no way that I could ever forget that laugh. I quickly got up from the table to follow the guy that had just got up heading toward the restroom. As I walked past the table, he had been sitting at someone grabbed my arm.

"Claire Walker right?" I nodded starting to walk away again but she pulled me back.

"I'm Alexia Hallford I called you earlier this week concerning your book?" I nodded looking around not sure whether to go after the guy who might be Xander or to stay and work on getting my book published.

"Yes." I finally answered turning to look at her.

"Well, sit down. We have tons to talk about." She gushed motioning to the seat that 'Xander' had just occupied.

"How did you get my book?"

"Let's not worry about that right now. Let's talk business."

"Well. What do you want to talk about?" I asked as a million questions began to run through my head.

"Well we already had your book printed so we plan on having a release party for it next week. We hope that it wasn't too forward, but we called your parents and they gave the ok after you didn't return any of our phone calls."

"Your name is Alexia, right?"

"Yes. Are you ok with us releasing your book next week? We promise we gave you the best deal possible for your book and we'll pay you as soon as you can get in and sign the contract."

"Sure, that sounds fine. Do you have a brother?"

"I don't see what that has to do with any of this, but yes I do."

"Claire what are you doing?" I looked up to see Sophie motioning for me to come back over to the table.

"Well it looks like your friends want you to come eat so stop by tomorrow and we'll go over all the details." I nodded as she shook my hand before walking out of the restaurant. I got up slowly and walked back over to my table where everyone was waiting in confusion.

"Who was that?" Allison asked as soon as I sat down.

"Alexia Hallford, she called me earlier about publishing my book. She wants me to come by tomorrow and sign the contract."

"What?!" Was the excited reply that came unanimously.

"Somehow she got a hold of my book and they printed it with my parent's permission. The release party is next week."

"That's amazing!" Sophie pulled me into a tight hug as everyone else gave their excited congratulations. I sat back down in my chair glancing around trying to see if I could see the guy again.

"Who do you keep looking for?" My head snapped around to see Jason staring at me intently.

"Oh she's probably trying to find her lover boy." Allison cried out in pain as I kicked her in her shin, glaring at her along with Sophie.

"What do you mean?" Jason asked his eyes not leaving me.

"It's nothing could you just drop it." I snapped harsher than what I meant it to be.

"Is it that guy who kidnapped you?" Brad asked staring intently at his plate.

"He didn't kidnap me!" I yelled jumping up from the table.

"He left you Claire, and yet you're still wearing his jacket?!" Jason had jumped up as well, causing me to step back.

"I bet you didn't get like this over us!" Brad had jumped up now as well.

"I love him!" I screamed causing everyone who hadn't been staring at us start to.

"Just like you loved us?!" Jason screamed back.

"SIT DOWN!" Sophie yelled causing us all to turn toward her ending our glaring match. I immediately complied as well as Jason and Brad. Sophie yelling was a scary thing.

"Now you are all going to listen to me and I don't want to hear one word out of any of you. Claire loved you two, but she's in love with Xander. Let her be, and let's all celebrate her upcoming book, like the friends that we are supposed to be." We all sat quietly as she stared each of us down until we all had nodded in agreement. Derek started to chuckle but Sophie whipped around causing him to cease his laughter, and look down at his plate as if it was the most interesting thing in the world.

"Let's all do as my lovely wife says and celebrate." Derek finally said raising his glass in a toast. We all raised our glasses as well toasting to my upcoming book. I looked across the table at Jason and Brad to see them lower their head in shame.

"TO CLAIRE!" I placed a smile on my face as everyone at my table started to toast each other. I glanced back over across the table to see both Brad and Jason mouth 'I'm sorry' a pleading look in their eyes. I lowered my gaze and nodded trying to understand what they must have gone through during this entire time. I raised my eyes to meet theirs and smiled letting them know I had forgiven them. I was going to start a new life here in Colorado and it started now with forgiving my ex-boyfriends.

Epilogue

Here is the author of the soon to be bestseller 'Home Isn't Always Where the Heart Is', Claire Walker!" I walked onto the stage taking the microphone from Alexia. I waited for the applause to die down in the party hall before I spoke.

"Thank you so much for all of your support. I don't know what I would've done without each and every fan who has pre-ordered my book. In addition, I would like to thank my friends and family who have been with me throughout this entire thing even if it was only in spirit. Alexia, there are not enough words to describe how thankful I am for this opportunity that you are giving me. I hope you all enjoy reading it!" I smiled brightly as I walked off the stage hugging Sophie who couldn't stop jumping up and down from excitement.

"Sophie calm down." I laughed as Derek gave me a hug also laughing at his wife's antics.

"By the way she's acting you would think she's the one with the best seller." I turned to see Allison walking toward us.

"Are my parents coming?"

"They said they would be if your mom was feeling well enough to travel." I nodded, my shoulders sinking slightly in disappointment. I glanced around the crowded room for Alexia to see her standing in a corner with the same guy I had saw her with that night at the restaurant. Jason, Brad, Ben, and Elizabeth then walked into my view congratulating me on my accomplishment. I quickly thanked them trying to keep Alexia and the guy in my sight. I excused myself before walking away toward Alexia and the guy.

"Claire!" I stopped and turned to see my parents standing behind me smiling.

"Mom, Dad!" I exclaimed running over to them temporarily forgetting the guy.

"We are so proud of you Claire." My mom beamed as happiness seemed to radiate off her and my father both.

"You are?!" I asked not bothering to hide my shock.

"Of course we are. You are our daughter and you just made a huge accomplishment." I smiled brightly not wanting to argue or ruin the happiness I was feeling at this very moment. I hugged my parents tightly, savoring this moment that would be one I would remember forever. This was the first time my parents had actually been proud of something I had done on my own accord. I glanced behind me as my parents continued to tell me everything that had happened since I had left. I saw the guy turn toward me and walk hastily in the opposite direction.

"Excuse me." I hugged my parents once more before running after the guy. I ran through the doors out into the foyer to see him start down the steps toward the exit.

"XANDER!" I yelled in a last attempt to get him to notice me. I saw him pause and turn toward me. My eyes widened as I began to run toward Xander as fast as I could in heels.

"Whoa Blondie calm down." I stood at the top of the steps not wanting to believe Xander was actually standing before me. The shock quickly passed though and was replaced with anger and questions.

"Why did you leave me? Did you steal my book? Your father owns Hallford publishing company! Alexia is your twin sister! Why didn't you tell me any of this? What were you thinking?!" I was cut off as Xander closed the gap between us and bringing me into a breathtaking kiss. I slowly let my eyes flutter close as I melted into the kiss and his arms once more.

"Shut up, Blondie," he said huskily, as he pulled back from the kiss smirking. I smirked back, before pulling him back into another breathtaking, life-altering kiss.

CPSIA information can be obtained at www.ICGtesting.com
Printed in the USA
BVOW02s1022090315

390879BV00001B/114/P